'Yo…

observed.

'I'm not going to ju…

'I—I never thought for one minute that you were,' she stuttered.

'No?' he said dryly. 'Kate, I kissed you once and you told me you didn't enjoy the experience. I have no intention of kissing you again until you tell me that you want me to.'

She noticed he hadn't said he wouldn't ever kiss her again, and warm colour spread across her cheeks. 'Ethan—'

'Kate, if I'd intended having my wicked way with you I certainly wouldn't have planned a long and tiring car drive first, nor would I have brought my daughter along as a spectator.'

Maggie Kingsley lives with her family in a remote cottage in the north of Scotland surrounded by sheep and deer. She is from a family with a strong medical tradition, and has enjoyed a varied career, including lecturing and working for a major charity, but writing has always been her first love. When not writing, she combines working for an employment agency with her other interest, interior design.

Recent titles by the same author:

IZZIE'S CHOICE

FOR JODIE'S SAKE

BY
MAGGIE KINGSLEY

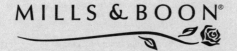

MILLS & BOON®

MILLS & BOON and MILLS & BOON with the Rose Device are registered trademarks of the publisher.

First published in Great Britain 2000
Harlequin Mills & Boon Limited,
Eton House, 18-24 Paradise Road, Richmond, Surrey TW9 1SR

© Maggie Kingsley 2000

ISBN 0 263 82229 X

Set in Times Roman 10½ on 11¼ pt.
03-0004-53901

Printed and bound in Spain
by Litografia Rosés, S.A., Barcelona

CHAPTER ONE

IT WAS obvious even from across the crowded restaurant that Andrew was angry. He was wearing one of his tight-lipped looks—the look which always heralded one of his 'I'm only telling you this for your own good' speeches, and Kate's heart sank. Now she knew why he'd invited her to lunch. Phyllis must have phoned him right away and he'd decided the situation called for a big brother chat.

'Is it true?' he demanded before she'd even sat down. 'You've taken a private nursing job in Manchester, looking after some retired GP?'

Trust their aunt to get it all wrong, Kate thought wryly, and trust Andrew to think it was any of his business in the first place.

'Ethan Flett was a consultant cardiologist in Harley Street before he retired four years ago,' she replied evenly. 'He lives near Alnwick in Northumberland, and it's his daughter I'll be looking after, not him.'

She'd thought the mention of Harley Street might take the wind out of her brother's sails, and it did. Andrew had always been a bit of a snob but since he'd been made a partner in his accountancy firm he'd undoubtedly got worse.

'So what's wrong with Dr Flett's daughter?' he asked, slightly mollified.

'Jodie has cystic fibrosis.'

He frowned. 'That's some sort of lung disease, isn't it?'

'It's actually an inherited condition which affects the glands that produce body fluids, causing them to produce much thicker fluids than normal. Without constant physiotherapy and drugs, these thicker fluids damage the lungs and the pancreas—'

Her brother's deep groan stopped her in her tracks. 'In other words, it's a life-threatening disease. Oh, for God's sake, Kate, didn't you go through enough with Simon two years ago, without taking on a patient like that?'

Her heart contracted with a jolt of pain. Two years. How could it have been two years since Simon died? Sometimes it felt like a lifetime, sometimes it felt like only yesterday.

'I have to work, Andrew,' she murmured, blinking back the tears which still surfaced far too easily whenever she thought about her husband.

'If Simon had listened to me, and taken out life insurance when you got married, you wouldn't *have* to do anything,' he declared, waving aside the hovering waiter with irritation. 'You're in a mess financially, aren't you?'

She was. She'd never grudged giving up her post at the Birnham Infirmary to nurse Simon at home. It had been what they'd both wanted, and she wouldn't have had it any other way, but it had left her massively in debt, though not for the world would she ever have told her brother that.

'I'm fine, Andrew,' she lied. 'I just like nursing—I always have.'

'Then why don't you go back to the Birnham?' he demanded. 'In fact, you should have gone back there after Simon died, instead of taking all those temporary supply jobs, and I'll never understand why you didn't.'

No, you wouldn't understand, she thought as she gazed at her brother's puzzled face. You wouldn't understand because you don't feel sick every time you pass the hospital, remembering the day the leukaemia was diagnosed, the day your whole world fell apart.

'I needed a change of scene,' she replied with an effort. 'I still do.'

'But Phyllis said you haven't even met this Ethan Flett. The whole interview was conducted by phone.'

'Dr Flett writes medical books now he's retired and he doesn't like being away from home—'

'And his wife?' he interrupted tartly. 'Doesn't she like being away from home either?'

She stirred uncomfortably in her seat. Andrew's voice only ever operated on two levels—loud and strident—and it was most definitely strident today, judging by the curious glances of the other diners.

'His wife's dead, Andrew,' she murmured. 'He's a widower.'

Andrew frowned. 'Hang on a minute. If he's a retired widower, how old is this daughter?'

'She's fourteen.'

Her brother's eyes rolled heavenwards. 'In other words, the guy married late, and now his kid's getting to that difficult age he's looking for someone to dump her on.'

'No, he's not,' she protested, wondering why she should feel so protective of someone she'd never met. 'In fact, I thought he sounded rather nice on the phone.'

Actually, she'd thought he'd sounded very nice on the phone. A big man in his late sixties, she imagined, big and solid with perhaps the beginnings of a paunch and a slightly receding hairline. The kind of man who'd wear woolly sweaters and baggy corduroys and play golf on Saturdays.

'"I thought he sounded rather nice on the phone,"' Andrew mimicked in exasperation. 'Honestly, Kate, there are times when I despair of you. You've taken a job with a man you've never met, in a house you've never seen, in a part of the country you've never visited. Ethan Flett could be the boss from hell for all you know, and as for his daughter… You haven't worked in paediatrics for years. You're a trained theatre sister, for heaven's sake…'

Why am I taking this? she wondered, as her brother launched into a dire account of the problems she'd undoubtedly face. I'm not a child. I'm twenty-nine years old So why am I just sitting here, taking this?

Because I'm tired, she realised—bone-achingly, mind-numbingly tired. Because right now it's far easier to let Andrew's words wash over me than argue with him, and because in five days' time I'll be in Northumberland and Andrew can do whatever he damn well likes with his opinions.

'You're not even listening to me, are you?' her brother exclaimed. 'Well, don't come crying to me if you end up looking after some spoilt brat twenty-four hours a day, seven days a week. And don't blame me if Ethan Flett makes Attila the Hun look like Noddy, and his home is some damp-ridden mausoleum stuck out in the middle of nowhere!'

'Well, you were half-right about the house, Andrew,' Kate murmured as the taxi driver drove away, leaving her standing on the wide stone steps in front of Malden Manor. 'It's certainly stuck out in the middle of nowhere, but a damp-ridden mausoleum it most definitely isn't.'

In fact, Ethan Flett's home was one of the loveliest Georgian houses she'd ever seen, and she was suddenly terrified.

'Pull yourself together, woman,' she told herself severely as she leaned forward and pressed the doorbell. 'So the house is massive and you feel like a poor relation, begging for shelter. So you know scarcely anything at all about Dr Flett or his daughter. He wouldn't have hired you if he hadn't thought you were right for the job.'

And she did want to be right for it, she realised as she breathed in deeply, savouring the sweet scent of the many roses edging the immaculately manicured lawn. At first, when she'd seen the post advertised, it had simply seemed like the answer to her prayers—a well-paid nursing position far away from London and her memories—but now she was here... Already she could feel the hard knot of tension be-

tween her shoulder blades easing, the knot that had been
there ever since—

'Sister Rendall?'

She whirled round quickly to see a tall young man regarding her uncertainly, and fixed a smile to her lips. 'Dr
Flett—'

'Afraid not.' He grinned. 'I'm Martin Letham—Dr
Flett's secretary.'

She bit her lip. Of course he wasn't Ethan Flett. He was
much too young for a start, and his voice was all wrong.
The voice on the phone had been deep, and velvety, and
oddly comforting.

'You *are* Sister Rendall, I take it?' he pressed.

She nodded and saw his grin deepen.

'Boy, but somebody's sure in for a big surprise,' he muttered under his breath, picking up her suitcase and leading
the way into the house.

'A surprise?' she echoed, following him.

That the secretary had never intended her to hear his
comment was plain. Clear consternation appeared on his
face and a dull flush of colour crept up his neck. 'Just
talking to myself, Sister.'

'But…' The rest of what she'd been about to say died
in her throat and Martin's grin reappeared as she stared in
awe at the hallway's marble floor, the huge portraits on the
walls and the wide stone staircase which simply screamed
out for someone wearing a gorgeous ball gown to come
sweeping down it.

'Malden gets everyone like that first time,' he observed.
'Try thinking of it as being just like your own home only
bigger.'

He had to be joking. The dingy little rented flat she'd
been forced to move into after Simon's death was nothing
like this, and it wasn't merely a question of scale.
Unconsciously she shook her head. Working in private

medicine sure beat the hell out of the NHS when it came to financial reward.

'The house isn't Dr Flett's,' the secretary said, as though he'd read her mind. 'It belonged to his wife's family, and when Mrs Flett died it was left in trust to Jodie.'

She knew it shouldn't have mattered to her how Ethan Flett had acquired a house like this, yet she couldn't deny she was pleased to hear that the owner of the velvety voice hadn't bought Malden with the proceeds from his private practice.

'It must take an army of people to look after a house this big,' she commented as she followed Martin across the hall, then down a series of bewilderingly similar corridors.

'It would if Dr Flett entertained but he never does. There's just the cook, Rhona Mathieson, Ted Burton who takes care of the garden, and a couple of girls who come in once a week to clean.'

'That's all?' Kate gasped. 'Good grief, either you've got Jodie and her friends very well organised or they're pretty unique teenagers.'

'Jodie's friends?' Martin repeated in confusion.

Kate chuckled. 'In my experience it doesn't take the average teenager more than ten minutes to turn a house into something resembling a bomb site!'

The secretary looked suddenly uncomfortable. 'We don't have that problem at Malden. Jodie…she doesn't have any friends.'

Kate's jaw dropped. 'Jodie doesn't have—?'

'The boss is in here,' Martin interrupted, opening the door beside him with clear relief. 'And I'm sure he'll be pleased to answer any questions about his daughter.'

He'd better be, Kate thought grimly, but the minute she strode into the huge, book-lined study all thoughts of asking her new employer anything—far less demanding to know why his daughter didn't have any friends—promptly disappeared.

Where, oh, where, she wondered with dismay, was the portly, balding man in his late sixties she'd so fondly imagined from Ethan Flett's voice on the phone? The man standing beside the desk possessed a physique any weightlifter would have been proud of, a shock of brown hair that could have been used in shampoo advertisements and, far from being anywhere near retirement age, she very much doubted whether he'd even left his late thirties behind.

The one thing she'd been right about was his height, she realised as he advanced towards her in a pair of hip-hugging denims and matching shirt, but at least he looked as friendly as he'd sounded on the phone, and he was smiling…

Correction. He had been smiling, but now his smile had gone. What on earth was wrong? she wondered, seeing dismay appear in his startlingly blue eyes. Did she look even more dishevelled than she felt after so many hours on the train? Was there a hole in her tights, a smudge of dirt on her chin? What was so very wrong about her appearance that it could wipe the smile off his face in an instant?

Ethan Flett groaned inwardly as he gazed down at the girl standing in front of him. Where, oh, where, was the small, motherly woman he'd so fondly imagined from Kate Rendall's voice on the phone? She was small certainly, scarcely more than five feet tall, but, far from appearing motherly, she looked in serious need of some mothering herself.

He'd never seen anyone outside of a hospital bed who looked quite so white, and as for being thin…! He could see the clear outline of her collar-bone under her pink blouse, and the sharp jut of her hips beneath her navy blue skirt.

Swiftly he shifted his gaze back to her face and his heart sank still further. She looked like a puppy who'd been beaten and expected to be beaten again, and to his horror he found himself wanting to put his arm round her thin shoulders, to tell her he'd personally sort out the brute who had hurt her.

Get a grip, he told himself, pulling a chair forward for her quickly before retreating back behind his desk in case he should be tempted to put his thoughts into action. This girl—woman—is supposed to be here to look after Jodie, not for you to look after her. OK, a man could drown in those enormous brown eyes of hers. OK, she had the longest, curliest eyelashes he'd ever seen—but she'd never be able to cope with Jodie in a million years.

'Is there something wrong, Dr Flett?' she said hesitantly.

Her voice was deeper than it had been on the phone, deeper and softer, like water flowing gently over stones.

Like water flowing gently over stones? Lord, but he must be going nuts. Nobody—but nobody—thought in clichés like that nowadays and he couldn't for the life of him think why he suddenly had.

Quickly he pulled himself together. 'Sister Rendall, forgive me for being blunt, but you're much…you're not as robust as I had imagined.'

'Robust?' she repeated blankly.

He nodded. 'Taking care of a child with cystic fibrosis is no picnic, even for the fittest, and my daughter…' He shrugged ruefully. 'I'm afraid my daughter can be rather a handful at times.'

'Show me a teenager who isn't.' She smiled—a smile with curved lips that looked soft and moist and eminently kissable.

He was definitely going nuts, he decided, shifting uncomfortably in his seat. Feeling sorry for a far-too-thin woman with nothing to commend her but a pair of large brown eyes and a wealth of thick black hair cut into a shining bob, that was one thing. Finding her strangely attractive, that was something else.

He was so damned tired, that was the trouble. He

couldn't remember the last time he'd enjoyed a decent night's sleep, and he'd been so hoping Sister Rendall would take some of the burden off his shoulders. Not that Jodie was a burden—God forbid—but she was certainly a worry, and now it looked as though he'd simply landed himself with another one.

'Dr Flett, is there a problem?'

Too right there was, he thought, all too aware from the deepening colour on Kate Rendall's cheeks that he'd been staring at her in complete silence for far too long.

'Of course not,' he replied heartily. 'It's just…'

'Yes?' she prompted, sitting slightly forward in her seat.

An intriguing blend of summer roses and irises wafted towards him, and to his acute annoyance he found himself leaning towards it.

This was ridiculous, he told himself, determinedly sitting further back in his seat. He should be trying to figure out a way to get rid of this woman, not wasting time trying to identify her perfume. And he did need to get rid of her. Jodie would run rings round her in no time.

Rings. *Rings*, his brain repeated as his gaze fell on Kate Rendall's hands. She was married, and married meant there could yet be a way out of this mess.

'I did explain to you, didn't I, Sister, that the accommodation here is only suitable for a single person?' he said quickly. 'Your husband—'

'I'm a widow, Dr Flett.'

He bit his lip. He should have known. He should have recognised the haunted look about her face, the bruised look in her eyes. His own face had borne the same tell-tale scars when Gemma had died.

How was he going to get rid of her now? It would be like kicking somebody when they were down. He was stuck with her—at least in the short term. Stuck with a woman who didn't look as though she could say boo to a goose, far less control a wayward teenager, and all he could do was hope she'd realise it before he had to sack her.

With a sigh he reached into his desk. Martin had warned him of the dangers of hiring someone he'd never seen, but none of the nurses he'd met and hired over the past four years had stayed longer than six months. This time he'd decided to trust to instinct. Unconsciously he shook his head. So much for instinct.

'I worked out this regime for Jodie four years ago,' he declared, reluctantly extracting a file from his desk. 'It's pretty detailed but as it seems to suit her condition I'd prefer you didn't deviate from it in any way.'

She glanced through the notes then up at him, obviously puzzled. 'I thought you said your daughter was fourteen, Dr Flett?'

'She'll be fifteen next month on the twenty-sixth of July.'

'Then why isn't she doing her own physio? In a couple of years time she could be going to college, getting a job—'

'Neither alternative is likely, given her condition,' he interrupted smoothly. 'And if you do her physio I'll be sure it's being done properly.'

'But—'

'Sister Rendall, my daughter is far too young to be given such responsibility.'

She opened her mouth and closed it again, and he wondered what she'd been about to say. Instinct told him he wouldn't have liked it, and as she consulted his notes again and a small frown creased her forehead he knew she'd found something else in his notes he wasn't going to like either.

'There doesn't seem to be any time allotted in this…this regime for social visits, excursions,' she observed.

Was the woman stupid? he wondered. Her CV hadn't suggested it but, then, CVs could be highly selective, as he very well knew. 'Jodie has cystic fibrosis—'

'Which doesn't mean she should be either friendless or a hermit,' she broke in tartly.

His eyebrows rose. So Kate Rendall could say boo to a goose, could she? Well, he was delighted to see she actually possessed some backbone, but that didn't mean he was going to allow her to argue with him over Jodie's treatment. Feeling sympathetic towards her, that was one thing, but if he discovered she was ignoring any of his instructions she'd find herself back in London, widow or no widow.

'I think you'll find Jodie a remarkably self-contained teenager,' he declared with an edge. 'She has her books, and her drawing, and does not feel the need for company. Now, if you'll excuse me,' he continued, getting abruptly to his feet as she opened her mouth, 'I just have to make a phone call, then I'll show you to your accommodation.'

Kate waited only until the study door was safely closed behind him before letting out the angry breath she'd been holding.

He'd been trying to get rid of her. All that rubbish about her not being robust enough, and his daughter being difficult. He'd taken one look at her, had decided he hadn't liked what he'd seen, and he'd been trying to get rid of her.

Well, she wasn't going anywhere, she decided furiously. She needed this job, and it sounded as though Jodie needed her. My daughter's self-contained, he'd said. My daughter doesn't feel the need for company.

'Rubbish!' she exclaimed to the empty room.

All teenagers needed company. It helped them to grow, to mature, and if he was too much of an old stick-in-the-mud...

And he wasn't even old, she thought belligerently. How could he be retired? He was far too young to be retired—not to mention being far more attractive than any man who was the father of a teenage girl had any right to be.

And he was attractive. He might not possess the chocolate-box good looks of a film star, but he had a nice face, and a nice smile when he chose to use it, and as for those eyes of his...

Not that his eyes and his smile mattered a hill of beans to her, she told herself abruptly. Good grief, why should they? There would never be room in her heart for anyone but Simon, but she couldn't deny she would have felt a lot more comfortable with a man who was older, a man who was less...less...

'Ready, Sister Rendall?'

Lord, but the man must walk like a cat, she thought, spinning round, red-cheeked, to see Ethan Flett standing behind her.

'Is there something wrong?' he asked, his deep blue eyes fixed on her curiously.

Everything—just about everything, she decided—but managed to smile. 'Not a thing, Dr Flett.'

For one awful moment she thought he was going to press the point, then to her relief he turned on his heel and led the way out of his study and back along the maze of corridors.

'Rhona's put you next door to Jodie,' he said as they climbed the sweeping staircase. 'I'm hoping she won't ever need you during the night, but...'

He left the rest of his sentence unfinished and Kate nodded.

It was a well-known fact that a child with CF could go to bed apparently perfectly fit, and then suddenly have a bad attack for no apparent reason.

'These are your quarters,' he continued as he turned right at the top of the stairs and came to a halt. 'I hope they're satisfactory.'

She just managed to choke down her involuntary gasp as he ushered her into a large, sunny sitting-room and then through to an equally impressive bedroom and a small but perfectly appointed bathroom. Her quarters, as he'd called them, were a lot better than merely satisfactory but she managed to reply, 'They're very nice, thank you.'

'There's a tea- and coffee-maker if you want to make yourself a late-night drink—'

'And a fridge for my soft drinks.' She smiled. 'You seem to have thought of everything.'

'The fridge contains a duplicate set of my daughter's medications,' he said dryly. 'The other set is kept downstairs in the kitchen but I thought it wise to have some close at hand.'

Her cheeks burned. He must think her a complete fool but she'd honestly never been in a house this big before.

'While we're here I may as well introduce you to Jodie,' he went on, leading the way along the corridor to a door on which someone had pinned a large notice emblazoned with the words PRIVATE—KEEP OUT!

A smile appeared on Kate's lips—a smile that instantly disappeared when Dr Flett simply opened the door and walked straight in.

Unconsciously Kate shook her head. At almost fifteen Jodie was entitled to some privacy and it surely wouldn't have killed her father to have knocked and waited to be invited in.

The frail, blond-haired girl lying hunched over a book on the bed clearly thought the same. Her eyebrows rose at their entrance and then deliberately she turned her back on them.

'You could at least say hello to Mrs Rendall,' her father said, exasperation plain in his voice. 'And, for heaven's sake, sit up. I've told you time and time again that slumping is bad for your condition.'

For a moment the girl didn't move, then slowly—excruciatingly slowly—she swung her legs round to the floor. Kate sighed. Good posture was important for children with CF—it ensured the maximum intake of air to their lungs—

but nagging wasn't the way to achieve it. In fact, nagging was virtually guaranteed to achieve the opposite.

'I'm sorry we disturbed you,' she said gently. 'Is it a good book?'

A pair of defiant blue eyes met hers. 'If I ever get the chance to read it I'll let you know.'

An uncomfortable silence fell—a silence which was finally broken by Dr Flett awkwardly clearing his throat.

'Perhaps it might be better if I left the two of you alone to become better acquainted,' he said.

Kate's heart sank. She and Jodie would have to get to know one another eventually but did it have to be now when she felt so tired? Did it have to be now when she didn't have a clue as to how she was going to pierce the armour of the girl who was gazing so sullenly at her?

'I think that's a good idea, don't you, Jodie?' he continued. 'It would give you and Mrs Rendall a chance to talk—'

'Yeah, right,' his daughter interrupted. 'I can tell her about my CF and she can tell me about all the people she's nursed who suffered from it. Real scintillating stuff.'

'*Jodie!*'

'Well, what else do you expect us to talk about?' she demanded as her father's eyebrows snapped down. 'The EU, the current situation in the Gulf? I don't know her, and she doesn't know me. My illness is the only thing we've got in common.'

A deep flush of angry colour appeared on Ethan Flett's cheeks and Kate stepped forward quickly.

'I think leaving us alone is an excellent idea,' she said with considerably more confidence than she felt—a confidence which totally evaporated when Jodie immediately slumped back down on the bed the minute her father had gone.

Quickly Kate glanced round the room, looking for something—anything—that might give her an opening with the girl. Dr Flett had said his daughter liked drawing, but she didn't—at least not in the conventional sense. The sketches which covered every available surface in the bedroom weren't of people or places, but of clothes. Jodie's passion was for designing clothes and she was good—very good.

'You have real talent, Jodie,' Kate observed, picking up one of the drawings and gazing at it in admiration.

Without a word the girl leapt to her feet, pulled the drawing from her fingers and tore it in two. 'It's rubbish,' she said flatly.

The design had been stunning and it took all of Kate's self-control not to protest at its wanton destruction, but she knew better than to rise to the bait.

'If you say so.' She shrugged.

A surge of furious anger appeared in the girl's large blue eyes. 'Why don't you just go away? I don't *want* you here! I don't *need* you here! I may have CF but that doesn't mean I need a nursemaid!'

Her breathing was much too wheezy, her cough far too pronounced, and Kate nodded. 'I don't think you need one either.'

'Then what are you doing here?' Jodie demanded, tossing her long blond hair back from her shoulders.

'I think I'm here for your father.'

The girl gazed at her in bewilderment for a moment, then panic suffused her thin face. 'You mean he's ill…there's something wrong with him?'

'No, I don't mean that,' Kate said quickly. 'Look, do you mind if I sit down? It's hours since I left London and I'm absolutely shattered.'

Swiftly Jodie pulled forward a chair. 'OK. What do you mean, you think you're here for my father?'

'I think he wants me as a safety net,' Kate declared as she sat down. 'Oh, I'm sure he knows you could do your own physio, be trusted to take the right pills, and would tell him if you were having a bad day, but he's a worrier.

It's not enough for him to be able to lift the phone and get your doctor. He needs someone on the spot to make him feel safe.'

Jodie chewed her lip thoughtfully. 'That makes sense. But you're wrong about the physio. I couldn't possibly do it myself.'

For a second Kate hesitated. Dr Flett had been insistent she must always do his daughter's physio, but he was wrong. If Jodie never learned she'd never become independent, and everyone had that right—everyone.

'You're going to have to learn if you want to go to design college,' she found herself saying.

'Oh, get real,' the girl retorted scornfully. 'I'll never go to design college. I've got CF.'

'Which affects your lungs, not your hands or your eyes,' Kate declared firmly. 'The one thing you need is talent— and you've clearly got bucket-loads of that.'

Real interest flared for a moment in Jodie's face, then her lip curled. 'Oh, I get it. Show an interest in the poor little thing's hobby and that'll keep her sweet. Well, you can forget it, Mrs Rendall. I stopped believing in fairy tales years ago!'

And with that she threw herself back down on the bed and pointedly reopened her book.

Kate sighed as she got to her feet. Convincing Ethan Flett's daughter that she could do anything she wanted to wasn't going to be easy, but she'd always relished a challenge, and maybe in time…

What time? a little voice demanded at the back of her mind. Dr Flett's already made it plain he thinks you're a waste of space.

Then I'll convince him he's wrong, she argued back. I'll convince him I'm exactly the kind of nurse his daughter needs.

'Mrs Rendall?'

Kate turned to see Jodie regarding her with a slight frown.

'What you just said—about me doing my own physio, and maybe going to design college. Were you on the level? I mean, do you really think I could?'

'Frankly, I reckon you're probably cussed enough to be able to do anything if you really put your mind to it,' Kate replied with feeling.

A reluctant grin lit up the girl's face.

'OK, I'll think about it,' she declared. 'I still don't believe it's possible,' she added swiftly as Kate's lips curved with delight, 'but I'll think about it, OK?'

'OK.' Kate nodded gravely, damping down her smile with difficulty.

But her elation didn't last long. The minute she was standing outside in the corridor a rueful groan broke from her lips. So much for proving to Ethan Flett that she was just the kind of nurse he needed. Within minutes of meeting his daughter she'd not only suggested teaching her how to do her own physio, she'd also told her she could go to college if she wanted. When he found out he'd hit the roof.

'Sister Rendall!'

The wretched man *did* walk like a cat, she thought with dismay, turning to see Jodie's father striding towards her.

Tell him about the physio and design college before his daughter does, the little voice at the back of her mind said urgently, and she had opened her mouth to do just that when he forestalled her.

'Was she very rude to you?'

There was genuine concern on his face, but there was also something else. There was the exhaustion of a man who was perilously close to the breaking point, and an unexpected wave of sympathy swept over her.

'She's a teenager,' she said softly. 'It's obligatory.'

He sighed. 'If you say so.'

'Dr Flett—'

'That reminds me,' he interrupted. 'I know I told you on the phone that I didn't want you to wear a uniform because I don't think it's healthy for Jodie to be constantly reminded of her condition, but I don't think I said I'd rather we were on first-name terms. All this ''Sister Rendall'' and ''Dr Flett'' stuff—it smacks too much of hospitals. I'd prefer to call you Kate—and you must call me Ethan.'

'E-Ethan?' she stammered.

His dark eyebrows rose. 'You have a problem with that?'

'N-no, of course I don't have a problem,' she replied, but she did.

She didn't want to call him Ethan. She wanted to call him 'sir' or 'Dr Flett', something—anything—that would establish and maintain a professional barrier between them. Quite why that should seem so important to her she didn't know, but it did.

'Now, unless there's anything else you'd like to ask me concerning your duties,' he said, 'I'll leave you to get settled in.'

Tell him about the physio and design college, the little voice insisted, but she didn't.

Chicken, her mind said scornfully as she watched him walk away.

'Realist, more like,' she muttered. 'If I'd told him he'd have bounced me out of here so fast my feet wouldn't even have touched the floor.'

And she didn't want to be bounced out. Jodie needed her, despite all her protestations to the contrary, and as for Ethan Flett...

He clearly thought he'd made a big mistake in hiring her. But he was a writer, and writers spent a lot of time in their rooms, writing, didn't they? So with any luck she'd hardly see him.

Strangely that thought didn't give her nearly as much pleasure as she'd imagined it would, and she shook her head as she made her way along to her room.

She was tired, that was the trouble. Tired, and just a little bit emotional. Once she'd had a good night's sleep she'd be overjoyed at the prospect of hardly ever seeing her new employer, instead of feeling oddly and inexplicably disappointed.

CHAPTER TWO

'IT'S no use, Kate—I can't do it.'

'Yes, you can, Jodie. Just lie still and relax—'

'I *am* lying still, and I *am* relaxing, but nothing's happening!' the girl wailed. 'I did it yesterday, and the day before—why can't I do it today? You can't have taught me properly!'

'I have taught you properly,' Kate replied calmly, carefully adjusting the angle of the tipping bed to see if the increased gravity might help. 'Try again.'

Determinedly Jodie began clapping her hands against her thin chest to release the mucus trapped in her lungs, but Kate knew it was hopeless. The girl was becoming more and more exhausted by the second, and when tears of frustration appeared in her large blue eyes she caught hold of her hands quickly.

'OK, that's enough. Go back to the breathing control—I'll do the physio for you.'

'But—'

'One failure isn't a catastrophe, Jodie. It simply means you haven't had enough practice yet.'

The girl nodded reluctantly but when she began her breathing control Kate sighed under her breath.

There had been times during the past fortnight when she'd wondered at the wisdom of encouraging Jodie to do her own physio. The girl had to learn if she wanted to become more independent, but learning required patience, and patience was something Ethan Flett's daughter possessed very little of.

'You're still breathing too fast,' she observed as she placed her hands on Jodie's chest to see if she could feel any rattles or crackles in her lungs. 'Your tummy's only supposed to swell out a little bit when you breathe in, and then—'

'Sink down when I breathe out,' Jodie interrupted, her voice coming in uneven bursts as Kate rapidly began cupping her hands against her chest to loosen the secretions. 'I know.'

'Now—'

'Huff, cough and spit. I know—I *know*!' Jodie wheezed, spitting into the beaker Kate was holding out to her with distaste. 'God, how I hate this lousy disease. It's so... *gross*.'

'I know spitting isn't pleasant,' Kate said sympathetically, gently rolling the girl onto her other side, 'but it does clear your airways.'

'But people always think you've got some horrible contagious disease,' Jodie protested. 'When I went to school all the other kids thought it was disgusting and even the teachers looked the other way.'

It was true. People didn't mean to be cruel or unkind but coughing and spitting were regarded as such antisocial activities that it was very difficult to get people to accept there might be some medical reason behind it.

'Is that why you don't go to school any more?' Kate said gently. 'You found people's reactions embarrassing?'

'It's better, being taught at home,' Jodie mumbled into the tipping bed. 'Everyone at Malden understands.'

Everyone at Malden was far *too* understanding, Kate thought grimly, and Ethan was the worst. He shielded his daughter too much from the outside world and it wasn't healthy and it didn't help. The less Jodie saw of people the more afraid she'd become of their reactions to her condition, and Kate could see a time coming when she'd refuse to meet anyone outside her own little world.

'Huff, cough and spit for me once more,' she ordered. 'Good—that's great.'

'Is it OK?' Jodie asked, levering herself up on to her elbows to stare down at the mucus in the bottom of the beaker.

It wasn't any thicker or darker than normal and Kate smiled. 'It's fine—no sign of any infection at all. And it looks like you've got a visitor,' she added, hearing the sound of a car stopping outside the house.

Jodie rolled off the tipping bed and went over to the window.

'It's Aunt Di—my dad's sister!' she whooped with delight. 'Come on, I'll introduce you to her,' she continued, making swiftly to the door as Kate began folding away the tipping bed.

'Later—I've got things to do here first.'

'But I want you to come with me now,' Jodie insisted, her blue eyes suddenly petulant.

'I'm sure you do,' Kate replied, 'but I've got your notes to update for Dr Torrance. He's coming next week for your three-monthly check-up, remember.'

'Yes, but—'

'Jodie, the quicker you let me get on with them, the quicker I'll be finished.'

The girl's jaw set and Kate held her breath. Two weeks of living at Malden had taught her that it didn't take much to transform Jodie from a likeable young girl into a spoilt, demanding brat, but far too many people had given in to Ethan Flett's daughter in the past and Kate had no intention of becoming one of them.

'I'll see you at lunch, then?' Jodie declared sulkily.

Kate shook her head. 'I'll have my lunch in the kitchen with Rhona today. Jodie, your father's bound to want to talk to his sister privately,' she went on as the girl opened her mouth, clearly intending to protest, 'and he can hardly do that when I'm around, can he?'

'But you always eat with us. Dad likes you to.'

He did, and Kate couldn't for the life of her think why.

A few discreet enquiries had revealed that none of the girl's other nurses had been asked to take their meals in the huge dining room and Kate could only suppose Ethan had ordered it to keep an eye on her.

If that had been his reason then he must be sorely regretting it, she thought wryly. All Jodie ever wanted to talk about was London fashion, and though Kate had tried to make it interesting, by recounting amusing tales of some of the more outlandish clothes she'd seen on the city streets, she knew he must be bored to tears.

'It's not as though you need me at lunch, Jodie,' she continued, seeing the girl's deep frown become a scowl. 'Rhona will make sure your meal is high in energy and rich in protein. All you need to do is take your vitamin supplements, drink plenty of fluid, and make sure you spread—'

'My pancreatic enzyme capsules throughout the meal to aid my digestion,' Jodie finished flatly.

'There you are—you don't need me.' Kate smiled.

'Maybe not,' the girl declared as she banged out of the bedroom, 'but I can tell you right now my dad's not going to like you having lunch in the kitchen.'

Well, tough, Kate thought belligerently. Bringing her notes up to date should only take her an hour at the most and after a quick lunch she'd actually have some time to herself. Some time to do whatever she liked in the sure and certain knowledge that Ethan Flett wouldn't—and couldn't—suddenly appear.

And he sure as heck made a habit of suddenly appearing, she thought with irritation as she reached for her notebook. In fact, for a writer, he seemed to spend precious little time actually writing and an awful lot of time 'dropping by' on her and Jodie.

Of course he drops by, her mind protested. He's a caring father, and you don't exactly prove yourself to be Mrs Efficiency when he's around, do you? If you're not knocking things over, you're dropping them, and if you're not dropping them, you're losing them. Yes, but I wouldn't be quite so clumsy and absent-minded if he didn't fluster me all the time, she countered.

How in the world can he possibly fluster you? her mind demanded. All he ever does is perch himself on the arm of a chair and talk about the weather, and the state of the garden, and Northumberland.

Yes, but it's the way he talks about them, the little jokes he makes, the way he smiles…

In other words, you find him attractive, her mind whispered.

Of course I find him attractive, she retorted. I'd have to be blind not to see he was attractive, but seeing it doesn't mean anything, seeing it doesn't mean…doesn't mean…

No? the insidious little voice mocked.

No! she replied, opening her notebook with a snap.

It actually only took three quarters of an hour to finish writing up her notes. A quick brush of her hair and she was ready to go downstairs, but she had just reached the landing when she saw Ethan striding up the stairs towards her, his face determined.

'What's this I hear about you having lunch in the kitchen today?' he demanded. 'Kate, you can't do this to me—you couldn't be so cruel!'

'Cruel?' she repeated, totally thrown.

'I've managed to hide in my study all morning, but I'll never get away with it for lunch!'

She opened her mouth, closed it again and shook her head in confusion. 'I think we'd better start this conversation again. Your sister's here—'

'My sister who only ever has two topics of conversation whenever she visits, and I don't want to hear either of them.'

A splutter of laughter came from her. 'You want a bodyguard.'

'And how!' he exclaimed. 'Kate, please—I'm begging you. Will you join us for lunch?'

She put her head to one side, as though carefully considering his question, then chuckled again at his worried expression. 'Of course I will. Not only do I have a brother I'd permanently avoid were it at all possible, I've always been a sucker for a sob story!'

You don't know how right you are, Ethan thought ruefully as he followed her down the stairs. It *was* a sob story, as anyone who really knew him would have pointed out. His sister Diana might possess all the finesse of a steamroller but he could deal with her with both hands tied behind his back if he really wanted to. The simple truth was that if Kate hadn't joined them for lunch he would have missed her.

And it didn't make any sense. He'd only ever insisted she share her meals with them because he'd been certain it would rid him of the disturbing impact of their first meeting. He'd discover she was extremely boring, or had some irritating habit that drove him crazy, and that would be that.

But he hadn't found her boring or irritating. Instead, he'd found her kind and funny, and he loved the cute way her nose wrinkled when she smiled, and…

And he was definitely going to have to get out more, he told himself as he suddenly realised that not only were his eyes running over the slim outline of her back and neat small bottom as she walked ahead of him across the hall, but his fingers were itching to do the same.

'No chance.'

'Um…ah…sorry?' he said hesitantly as Kate turned towards him, a frown in her brown eyes.

'You just muttered you should get out more, and I said I'd believe it when I saw it.'

Thank God that was all he'd said, he thought, feeling a scorching heat creep up the back of his neck. It was bad enough to be plagued with these crazy fantasies but to actually voice them...!

'Kate—'

'At last!' a tall, stoutly built woman with steel-grey hair boomed, throwing open the dining-room door. 'I was beginning to think you'd run away.'

'I was correcting some proofs, Di—'

'Not you, little brother,' the woman interrupted dismissively. 'You I can see any time. It's this girl here—Jodie's new nurse—I'm anxious to meet.' Her eyes flicked critically over Kate and she shook her head in disbelief. 'Good grief, my dear. You're nothing but skin and bone!'

'Di, I really don't think—'

'Of course you don't,' his sister continued, as a deep flush of embarrassed colour appeared on Ethan's cheeks. 'You haven't since you were a toddler. The girl's far too thin and I'm sure she doesn't mind me saying so, do you, dear?'

'Of course not.' Kate chuckled, quite unable to be offended by Diana's bluntness.

'There you are,' she observed triumphantly as Ethan shook his head at her. 'Kate hasn't taken offence so neither should you. Now, when are we going to eat? I could eat a horse and from the looks of Kate she needs to!'

True to her promise, Kate made sure Diana was given no opportunity to launch into any kind of detailed conversation with her brother. From the moment Rhona brought in the first course of smoked salmon on a bed of lettuce until she served coffee and home-made shortbread, she didn't stop talking for a minute.

But she couldn't keep it up for ever. The minute Jodie dashed up to her room to find a book her aunt professed an interest in seeing, Diana rounded on her brother.

'What's this I hear about you turning down the consultant's job at St Margaret's in Newcastle?'

'I've retired, Di.'

'Men of thirty-nine don't retire, Ethan,' she retorted, 'and certainly not cardiologists of your calibre. It's a waste of your talent and your time.'

'Wanting to stay home and take care of my daughter is a waste of my time?' he snapped, his blue eyes suddenly ice-cold.

'When Jodie quite clearly doesn't need you twenty-four hours a day, seven days a week, it is,' Diana declared evenly. 'And I'm sure Kate agrees with me.'

Kate's heart sank as two pairs of eyes swivelled round to her. Martin had told her of the pioneering heart bypass operations Ethan had been performing before he'd retired, and Jodie certainly didn't need him constantly by her side, but he was her boss and the last thing she wanted was to be seen taking sides against him.

To her relief it was Ethan who came to her rescue.

'What Kate thinks is immaterial,' he declared firmly. 'The decision is mine, and mine alone.'

'It wouldn't be so bad if the time you spent with Jodie was productive,' Diana protested, 'but the two of you live like hermits—never going anywhere, never seeing anyone—'

'Drop it, Di,' he said tightly.

'And when I think of the marvellous parties you and Gemma used to throw,' she went on, as though he hadn't spoken. 'The fancy-dress balls, the dinners—'

'Gemma is dead,' he interrupted, his face cold.

'And has been for four years,' she declared brusquely. 'You and Jodie, however, are very much alive. The girl needs company, Ethan, even if you don't,' she continued as his jaw tightened perceptibly. 'She's almost fifteen—'

'Which gives her plenty of time yet to be thinking about parties.'

'And what about this young woman here?' Diana demanded, pointing a plump, be-ringed figure at Kate. 'How

long do you suppose she'll be happy to stay at Malden with
only you and Jodie and your staff for company?'

'I really don't mind it being quiet,' Kate said quickly,
seeing Ethan's brows lower ominously.

And she truly didn't mind, she realised. Having been
born and brought up in London, she supposed she ought to
have missed the crowds, the buzz of a city, but she didn't.

'But surely you agree that Jodie should meet and mingle
with people of her own age?' Diana pressed, fixing her deep
grey eyes on her.

Kate agreed wholeheartedly, but how on earth could she
possibly say so? She already felt guilty about going behind
Ethan's back in teaching his daughter to do her own physio,
and to side with his sister against him now would only
make her feel worse.

'I think...' she began slowly, then sighed with relief as
Jodie appeared at the dining-room door. 'I think we'll have
to leave this conversation for another day. It's time for
Jodie's exercise.'

'Do I *have* to?' the girl protested. 'Can't I give it a miss
as Aunt Di's here?'

Kate shook her head. 'You've got to loosen the secretions in your lungs, and exercise is the best way to do it.
How about a quick game of tennis?'

'Tennis is boring,' Jodie exclaimed truculently. 'And you
don't play properly anyway. All you ever do is pit-pat the
ball about.'

'That is an extremely rude observation, young lady,'
Ethan said sharply. 'Apologise to Kate at once.'

'Why should I when I'm speaking the truth?' she retorted. 'And I don't want to play tennis—I hate tennis—
and I wish we didn't have a tennis court.'

'Well, we do have one, and you will use it, and you will
use it now,' her father replied in a voice that brooked no
opposition.

Kate groaned inwardly as Jodie's face set into even more

mutinous lines. The girl always made a fuss about doing any kind of exercise but she could have coaxed her round if her father hadn't put her on the defensive. Now she'd be lucky to get her to walk round the court, far less play a game.

'I'll give you a match, sweetheart,' Diana declared unexpectedly. 'I can't promise it will be Wimbledon standard but I'll certainly give you a run for your money. Always supposing I don't fall flat on my face in this straight skirt, of course,' she added with a comical wink.

Kate sent up a silent prayer of thanks as Jodie laughingly followed her aunt out of the French windows. Diana might be blunt to the point of rudeness but at least she understood teenagers, whereas her brother... Her brother seemed to possess the unfortunate and unerring ability to constantly put his daughter's back up.

'I'm in the dog-house, aren't I?' he said, turning round suddenly in his seat towards her.

'The dog-house?' she repeated in surprise.

His lips curved ruefully. 'If looks could have killed when I told Jodie she had to do her exercise, I'd be lying slumped over the Stilton now, but exercise is vital for her condition.'

'Yes, but...'

'But?' he prompted.

She stared down at her empty coffee-cup and wondered how she could possibly phrase what she wanted to say tactfully.

'You meant well, I know you did,' she said at last, 'but when you push Jodie into a corner like that, tell her she *must* do something, it...well...it doesn't help.'

All amusement vanished from his face. 'I see,' he said stiffly.

'I appreciate your help—please, don't think I don't,' she said hurriedly, 'but—'

'You'd rather I didn't help.'

His mouth had twisted and to her dismay she suddenly

felt an overwhelming desire to reach out across the table and squeeze his hand reassuringly.

What in the world had got into her? she wondered, gripping her coffee-cup tightly in case she should be tempted to put her thoughts into action. Ethan Flett wasn't her patient. He didn't need help—leastways not medical help—and any other kind of help was most certainly not part of her job description.

Talk about something else, her mind urged, talk about *anything* else—and fast.

'"When are you going back to work?" and "When are you going to stop living like a hermit?"' she said quickly. 'The two topics of conversation your sister always raises when she visits,' she added as he stared at her in clear bewilderment.

'Got it in one,' he replied with an attempt at a laugh that deceived neither of them. 'Di means well—I know she does—but, you see, if anything should happen to Jodie—something my presence could have prevented—I couldn't live with myself—I couldn't.'

But you're smothering her, she thought, gazing across at him. You're not letting her live her own life, make her own mistakes. You're so worried that you're going to lose her that you're giving her no independent life at all.

'There have been huge advances in the treatment of cystic fibrosis since Jodie was born, Ethan,' she began hesitantly. 'PEP masks from Denmark—'

'Heart and lung transplants, DNase to thin the mucus which clogs the lungs, gene therapy,' he finished for her, counting them off on his fingers. 'I'm a doctor, remember.'

'Yes, and as a doctor you should also know that the CF gene has been isolated,' she argued, 'and it's simply a question of time before a copy of a healthy gene can be inserted into the cell containing the faulty form to produce normal protein.'

"'Simply a question of time,'" he echoed. 'That's the trouble, isn't it? I don't know if Jodie has enough time.'

His face was impassive but there was such pain, such heartache, in his blue eyes that she had to swallow hard before she could answer.

'None of us can know for certain whether we have a future,' she replied, her voice low.

He glanced across at her sharply. She was thinking about her husband—he knew she was—and he found himself wondering how he'd died. He guessed it would be something sudden—unexpected—like a car crash, just as he also guessed that she rarely spoke about him and that she should.

Silently he refilled her coffee-cup and cleared his throat. 'Your husband... When did he die?'

That she hadn't expected the question was clear. Her head came up in surprise, then she said with an effort, 'Two years ago.' Two years, one month and three days ago, to be exact, she added mentally.

'It's the waking up in the morning that's the hardest at first,' he said softly. 'For a split second you don't remember they've died, and then suddenly you remember and the pain is as fresh and as sharp as it was on the first day.'

She nodded, her eyes clouded. 'And for the rest of the day, no matter what you do or where you go, everything reminds you of them.'

'Is that why you took this job?' he asked. 'You wanted to get away?'

'My brother—'

'The one you'd prefer never to see again?'

'The same,' she said with a shaky smile. 'He...my friends...they mean well, but...'

'The trouble is, nobody knows what to say,' he observed. 'My friends used to cross the street to avoid me in case I did something deeply embarrassing, like bursting into tears.'

'And if they don't cross the street they ask you how you are, and you end up telling them you're OK—'

'Not because you are but because you know that's what they want to hear,' he finished for her.

He understood, she thought with relief. So many people said that they did, but he actually did.

'Does it…?' She paused, feeling the familiar burn of tears in her throat. 'Does it get better with time?'

He hadn't thought it would. He had never thought it would, but now, sitting across from this girl, feeling the longing to take her in his arms and ease the pain he knew only too well, he knew that it did.

'It changes,' he murmured. 'The hurt's still there but gradually you find yourself able to remember the good times, and somehow…somehow it doesn't hurt so much any more.'

She couldn't imagine ever being able to think about Simon and not feeling pain, and he must have read her mind because he suddenly leaned across the table and caught one of her hands in his.

'Kate, listen to me—'

'Six–four!' Jodie exclaimed excitedly as she clattered through the French windows, her pale cheeks flushed, her blond hair dishevelled. 'I beat Aunt Di six–four and she didn't let me win—she really was trying to beat me!'

'Well done,' Kate replied, pulling her hand free from Ethan's jerkily, all too aware that her cheeks were as red as the girl's. 'Where's your aunt? She's not lying in a collapsed heap on the tennis court, is she?'

Jodie giggled and shook her head. 'She met Ted on the way back to the house and the last I saw she was giving him a lecture on the best way to prune roses.'

Ethan groaned. 'Kate, could you drag her away from him before he resigns? I'd do it myself but I'd better look out those books she wants to borrow, and if I don't do it now she'll still be with us at dinner.'

'I'll get her for you, Dad.'

'No, you won't,' he said firmly as Jodie half turned to go back out of the dining room again. 'You need to take some salt tablets after all that exercise.'

'I'll take them later.'

'*Jodie*—'

'OK, OK, I'll take them now,' she replied, sticking out her tongue at him as she went, 'but, honestly, Dad, you can't half be an old fuss-budget at times!'

Ethan winced as his daughter banged out of the dining room. 'My daughter the critic. You don't mind rescuing Ted for me, do you, Kate?'

She didn't. In fact, she was already halfway out of the French windows, knowing she didn't care where she went as long as it was as far away from him as she could possibly get right now.

She was losing her mind, she decided as she made her way down to the tennis court. Andrew had said she'd been insane to take this job and insanity was the only possible— plausible—explanation for the inexplicable desire she'd suddenly felt when Ethan had caught hold of her hand to throw herself onto his broad chest and sob out all the misery and heartache of the last three years.

He was her boss, for heaven's sake. You didn't throw yourself into the arms of your boss, but if Jodie hadn't come in…

She'd never allowed anyone to see her cry. Even with Simon—even when she'd known the end hadn't been very far away—she'd managed to keep her tears under control until he'd fallen asleep, and yet within the space of two short weeks of meeting Ethan Flett—

'Problems?'

It had to be inherited, Kate thought, whirling round, startled, to see Ethan's sister gazing at her curiously. This ability to creep up on people simply had to be inherited.

'Ethan—'

'Wants to know when the hell I'm leaving,' Diana finished for her. 'It's OK, dear.' She chuckled as Kate coloured. 'We rub each other up the wrong way—always have
done. I'm blunt and he's perverse—it's an explosive com-
bination.'

'It sounds it.' Kate could not help but laugh.

'I blame all those years he spent at St Finbars,' Diana
continued. 'Too many student doctors running round after
him, never daring to argue in case it looked bad on their
records. If no one ever argues with you, you start thinking
you're always right.'

'Dr Flett worked at St Finbars?' Kate said with surprise,
recognising the name of one of London's poorest and most
deprived inner city hospitals.

'For eight years. He only moved into private practice
when Jodie was seven so he could be home more with her
and Gemma.'

'What was she like—Gemma, I mean?' Kate asked. 'I've
heard she was beautiful, but what was she like as a person?'

'Lovely,' Diana said simply. 'Kind to a fault, a wonderful hostess and a terrific horsewoman. Which makes the
way she died all the more tragic.'

'It was a riding accident, wasn't it?' Kate said as she
began to lead the way back to the house.

Diana nodded. 'She was riding point-to-point when her
horse stumbled and threw her. She was killed instantly.'

'Jodie clearly loved her very much,' Kate murmured.

'And Gemma adored her. She was devastated when the
CF was diagnosed. She didn't know—not even Ethan considered the possibility—that they might both be the one in
twenty-five of the population who carry the cystic fibrosis
gene.'

'And as they were both carriers the chances of them having a CF child became one in four.' Kate sighed. 'I just
wish the government would introduce a nationwide screen-

ing programme. It's so easy to discover if you're a carrier—all it takes is one simple mouthwash test.'

'And I just wish my brother would go back to work,' Diana said angrily. 'This life he leads—working from home, rarely going out, never seeing anyone—it's not healthy.'

'Mrs Wilson—'

'I know, I know. He's your boss, and you don't want to get involved, but maybe you could make him see sense.'

'I couldn't persuade your brother to do anything, believe me,' Kate protested.

Diana's face creased into a warm smile. 'I think you could. In fact, I think you could do both my brother and Jodie a great deal of good.'

Kate couldn't see how, but as Ethan and Jodie were waving to them from the front of the house she had no opportunity to ask.

'Not very subtle, little brother,' Diana protested as Ethan opened her car door the minute she drew level with him.

'Simply thinking of you, Di,' he said, his face perfectly bland. 'It's a two-hour drive back to Harrogate, and you don't want to be late home for dinner.'

'A shade unlikely as it's just gone half past three.' She laughed, stretching up to kiss him lightly on the cheek. 'Take care of yourself, Ethan—you, too, Jodie. I'll see you again soon.'

'Is that a threat or a promise, Di?' Her brother grinned.

'Depends on your perspective,' she replied, her eyes dancing as she got into her car. 'Just try to get some weight on Kate before I see her again, OK?'

And with a wave of her hand, and a blast of her horn, she was gone.

'I like your sister,' Kate observed, turning to Ethan as Jodie disappeared into the house, clutching the huge bundle of fashion magazines her aunt had brought her.

'So do I. In very small and well-rationed doses.'

She chuckled, and so did he, then a slight frown appeared on his face. 'Kate—what Di said—about you being lonely here. Are you lonely?'

'Not a bit,' she answered truthfully.

'If you ever find you are,' he continued, 'take my car—go out, meet people.'

'Are you serious?' she gasped, her eyes sparkling at the thought of driving his gleaming BMW.

'I was wrong about you, Kate, and I don't mind admitting it,' he said awkwardly. 'I thought you'd never be able to cope with Jodie but she seems so much more positive about her condition since you came, and I can't thank you enough.'

In any other circumstances she would have been delighted by his praise but all she could feel was guilt. Guilt for having encouraged Jodie to deceive him about doing her own physio. Guilt because he thought well of her when—if he had but known the truth—he most certainly wouldn't.

Embarrassed and uncomfortable, she turned quickly to go back into the house, but in her haste to be gone she caught her foot on one of the stone lions guarding the door and would have fallen if Ethan hadn't reached out and caught her firmly.

'Hey, be careful,' he exclaimed. 'It's bad enough Di thinking I starve you, without you ending up with a broken leg as well!'

An involuntary chuckle sprang from her lips but as she placed her hands on his chest to steady herself all thoughts of laughing instantly disappeared. She could feel his skin warm through his shirt, the hard nub of a tiny nipple, and she knew exactly when his heartbeat accelerated because her own did the same.

Dear God, what was happening to her? she wondered as she slowly lifted her head to stare up at him, all too aware that her knees were suddenly trembling and her breath felt

tight in her chest. Simon had been her first—her only—
love, and her body shouldn't be responding like this to a
virtual stranger.

And it was responding, she knew it was. There was a
dull ache of longing deep in the pit of her stomach for the
man who was holding her close to hold her closer still. For
the gentle hands that were encircling her waist to slide up
her body, to touch and caress her, and it was wrong—
wrong.

'Kate—what is it, what's the matter?' he asked, bewildered, as she pulled herself out of his grasp and backed
away from him, red-cheeked and horrified.

'N-nothing,' she stammered. 'I—I have to go. Jodie…
her physio. I…I have to go!'

'Kate, wait a minute!'

But she didn't wait. She turned and ran into the house
as if all the demons in hell were after her.

CHAPTER THREE

'POTATOES, coffee, cheese, flour—'

Rhona tapped the end of her pen against her teeth reflectively. 'Are you wanting anything from the shops yourself, Kate?'

'Not unless they're selling cold air in Alnwick,' she groaned, easing back the collar of her blue shirtwaister from her neck as a trickle of sweat ran down between her shoulder blades.

'Aye, it's hot, right enough,' Rhona agreed, wincing slightly as she reached up to check the contents of the biscuit barrel.

'I really do wish you'd let me take a look at you.' Kate frowned. 'You've had that pain ever since I came to Malden.'

'It's nothing,' the cook replied dismissively, quickly closing the pantry door. 'At my age you've got to expect a few aches and pains.'

'You're not old,' Kate protested. 'You can't be any more than—'

'Sixty-two next birthday,' Rhona declared wryly. 'And, believe me, in this heat I feel every day of it.'

Kate shook her head and laughed. 'If you won't let me examine you, I could ask Ethan—'

'Absolutely not!' the cook interrupted in horror. 'Take my clothes off for the boss? No way—not ever!'

'He is a doctor, Rhona.'

'Would you do it?' she demanded. 'No, I didn't think you would,' she continued as Kate coloured. 'Good grief, I'd never be able to look the man in the face again if he'd seen my bits and pieces!'

'But—'

'I need to lose some weight, that's all.'

'But—'

'And if you breathe one word of this to him, I'll never speak to you again!'

Kate sighed. She could understand Rhona's reservations about allowing Ethan to examine her. Lord, just the thought of taking off her clothes for him was enough to make her feel even hotter under the collar than she already did, but something was wrong with the woman. Yes, she was overweight and, yes, it was unbearably hot, but there was something else—she was sure there was.

'You did say Dr Torrance was due at ten o'clock, didn't you?' Rhona said, glancing up at the kitchen clock.

Kate nodded. The cook had asked her the same question twice already that morning but she wasn't surprised. The entire household was on edge, waiting for the results of Jodie's three-monthly check-up—herself included since she'd noticed Jodie's sputum was a little darker than usual this morning.

'That'll be him now, then,' Rhona observed as they both heard the distant jangle of the front doorbell. 'And, please God he finds nothing wrong with the wee lassie.'

I'll second that, Kate thought silently as she went out to meet him.

'All in all, I'm very pleased with Jodie's general condition,' Dr Torrance observed as he sat with Ethan and Kate in the study some time later. 'Her weight's stable and there's no sign of diabetes or heart strain, which is always a worry with CF children. She has a slight infection—'

'How slight?' Ethan interrupted, sitting bolt upright behind his desk, his concern plain upon his face.

'Practically negligible.' Bill Torrance smiled reassuringly. 'In fact, I'd attribute it to this infernal heat we've been having.'

'What treatment would you advise?' Kate asked, reaching for her notebook.

'Bronchodilator drugs via a nebuliser before she has her chest physiotherapy, and then some antibiotics orally afterwards. Just make sure she breathes through the mouthpiece and not through her nose when she uses the nebuliser, and that should cure it.'

'And if it doesn't?' Ethan demanded.

'Kate can give her an IV course of antibiotics. You have a sharps bin for the disposal of syringes and needles, don't you?' Bill Torrance added, glancing across at her.

She nodded.

'What about her diet?' Ethan asked. 'Do you think we should increase her pancreatic enzyme intake?'

Bill Torrance frowned. 'She hasn't lost weight so her body must be absorbing the food she's been eating. What are her stools like, Kate?'

'Perfect. Not loose at all.'

'Then there's no need to change the dosage. Don't let her slack on the exercise. Yes, I know she won't want to do any in this heat...' he smiled as Kate groaned '...but she has to do some. We've got to keep the joints and muscles around her chest and shoulders supple.'

'You're absolutely certain the infection is minor, Bill?' Ethan asked, his eyes fixed on the other man as though trying to read his mind.

'Absolutely one hundred per cent certain,' he replied firmly. 'And now, if there's nothing else,' he added, getting to his feet, 'I have other patients to visit and I really must be going. Kate, could you come out to the car with me and I'll give you the extra antibiotics you'll need.'

She accompanied him outside but he had barely reached his car when he turned towards her, his face worried.

'What on earth has Ethan been doing lately? He looks dreadful.'

'I know he's behind with his latest book—'

'Which is going to be published posthumously if he carries on like this,' he fumed. 'Can't you persuade him to take a holiday, a complete break from everything?'

Kate gazed at him in amazement. First Diana, now Bill Torrance. Why did everyone assume she had some sort of special relationship with Ethan? She didn't have *any* kind of relationship with Ethan, apart from being one of his employees—and she was only one of those under sufferance.

'OK, OK, don't shoot the messenger,' Bill Torrance said after she'd demanded to know in no uncertain terms how he expected her to achieve that miracle. 'But I'm telling you this. If somebody doesn't get him to take a holiday soon, I'm going to be visiting two patients at Malden.'

Kate frowned as she watched him drive away. Ethan *was* looking pale and drawn, but how in the world could she possibly persuade him to take a holiday when she'd been doing her level best to avoid him for the past week?

You're going to have to stop trying to avoid him, she told herself severely. OK, so you almost made a fool of yourself with him when Diana was here. OK, so he somehow managed to make your body feel more alive in ten seconds than it has done for years. He doesn't know what happened and he never will unless you tell him.

And she certainly had no intention of ever doing that, she thought grimly as she walked back into the house.

'How's Jodie?' Martin asked, popping his head round his office door, his face anxious.

'Fine. She has a slight infection but it's nothing to worry about.'

The secretary smiled with relief. 'That should set the boss's mind at rest.'

Kate doubted it. Actually, she rather suspected that Ethan had grown so used to hearing bad news he probably thought Bill Torrance was keeping something from him.

She was right. The minute she walked into the study, Ethan fixed her with a penetrating stare.

'It is just a minor infection, isn't it?'

'Bill's more worried about you than he is about Jodie,' she replied, sitting down opposite him.

'I'm fine,' he said dismissively.

'I have never called a consultant a liar in my life,' she said, 'but you're anything but fine, Ethan.'

His lips curved unexpectedly. 'Touting for more business, Sister Rendall?'

'Just being sensible,' she replied. 'You need a holiday.'

He shook his head. 'I'm too busy.'

'Nobody's too busy to take a holiday.'

'I am,' he insisted, picking up the letter-opener on his desk and turning it round in his fingers.

He had fine hands, she noticed, surgeon's hands. Hands that were strong but which could be gentle, too, as she knew from personal experience. A shiver ran down her spine, a shiver which felt disturbingly like the caress of soft fingertips, and deliberately she dragged her gaze back to his face.

'Jodie was such a beautiful baby when she was born,' he murmured, the letter-opener lying forgotten in his fingers as he stared, unseeing, at the bookcases behind her. 'And perfect—everyone said she was perfect. She cried a lot, of course, and she didn't seem to put on weight like she should, but I thought it was simply colic.'

She didn't move, she didn't say a word. She just sat where she was, realising he needed to talk.

'And then one night she started to cough,' he continued. 'I'd never heard an adult cough like that, far less a three-month-old baby. Gemma and I drove like maniacs to the nearest A and E unit and they told us she had pneumonia. They also told us she had CF. All it took was one five-second sweat test and our whole world caved in.'

Kate leaned forward quickly in her seat. 'Ethan, she is OK. Bill said—'

'I heard what he said,' he broke in, his face taut. 'Sometimes I feel I've spent my entire damn life listening to experts.'

He looked so tired, so weary, that she desperately wanted to comfort him, but comforting him meant putting her arms round those broad shoulders. Comforting him meant touching him, and that she knew she couldn't—mustn't—do.

'I'd better go,' he said, getting to his feet with an effort. 'My publishers are expecting me in Newcastle and arriving late isn't exactly going to endear me to them—especially when they find out I need an extension to my deadline.'

Slowly he walked to the study door and she followed him with concern. 'Ethan, can I telephone them—tell them you can't make it?'

'Postpone the evil hour?' He shook his head. 'Better to get it over with.'

Despite all her resolve, she put her hand on his arm. 'Are you sure? I mean, are you OK?'

He gazed down at her, his blue eyes dark, a slightly twisted smile on his lips. 'Hey, I'm always OK. I have to be, don't I?'

No, you don't, she thought. No one has to be invincible. 'Ethan, listen…'

But he wasn't listening. He was already walking away, and a deep frown appeared on her forehead.

Bill Torrance was right. If Ethan didn't take a break soon he was going to be really ill, but telling him Jodie could manage perfectly well without him for a few weeks was one thing, convincing him of that fact was something else.

'Fool!' she muttered to herself as she left the study.

'You wouldn't be talking about our esteemed boss, would you?' Martin grinned, appearing without warning round the corner.

'How did you guess?' she said wryly. 'Honestly, Martin, there are times when that man would turn a confirmed teetotaller into an alcoholic!'

He threw back his head and laughed.

'I thought you were going to Hexham today?' she went on, noticing the papers in his hand as he fell into step beside her.

'I'm just on my way. Which means that with me in Hexham, Rhona and Ted in Alnwick and the boss away in Newcastle, you and Jodie can throw that wild party you've been planning,' he said, his eyes dancing.

'Chance would be a fine thing,' she groaned. 'Keeping Jodie amused and out of my hair for the rest of the day is going to be the sum total of my activity, believe me!'

That, and trying to figure out a way of sending her father off on a holiday he didn't want to take, she added mentally as Martin shook his head and laughed again.

'Eat up, Jodie.'

'Don't feel like eating.'

'Then force yourself,' Kate said firmly as Jodie pushed her lunch around her plate without enthusiasm. 'Rhona made it especially for you, and she'll be hurt if you don't eat it.'

'It's too hot to eat.'

'The quicker you finish your lunch, the quicker you'll get back to that design you were working on,' Kate pointed out.

'It's rubbish.'

'Then why don't you finish that book you were reading? You said it was a good one.'

'Don't feel like reading.'

Kate just managed to bite back the retort that she'd heard quite enough for one day of all the things Jodie didn't want to do, and maybe she might try to come up with something constructive instead. They were both hot and irritable, and even changing into shorts and T-shirts before lunch hadn't made either of them feel any cooler.

'Look, why don't we go out for a walk?' she suggested, collecting their plates and carrying them over to the sink.

'Rhona told me there's a river on the outskirts of the Malden estate. We could go there—take a picnic, maybe paddle a bit.'

'Only little kids go paddling,' Jodie said scornfully.

'So I'm a kid at heart,' Kate exclaimed. 'Humour me.'

For a second Jodie said nothing, then sighed. 'I suppose it *might* be fun. And it would be a lot cooler by water, wouldn't it?'

'Absolutely,' Kate declared, opening the fridge door before Jodie could change her mind. 'What would you like for this picnic of ours?'

'Jam sandwiches would be nice.'

'Jam sandwiches it is,' Kate said with a nod, taking out the butter and reaching for the bread bin. 'How about a few nuts as well, and some juice and crisps?'

'Smoky bacon?'

'What else?' Kate chuckled. 'Now, I just have to write a note to let everyone know where we've gone—'

'Why?' Jodie protested as Kate tore a piece of paper from the notebook by the kitchen phone. 'We're not little kids—we don't have to tell everyone where we are every minute of the day.'

'Of course we don't, but if I don't leave word Rhona will probably think we've been kidnapped and sold off to some Arab sheikh.'

'Sounds like a lot more fun than paddling,' Jodie commented, her blue eyes sparkling.

'For you it might be,' Kate declared, putting their picnic into a basket. 'You're young and pretty and would probably end up as his twenty-fifth wife. I'd end up stuck in some horrible kitchen, scrubbing pots and pans for the rest of my life.'

Jodie gazed at her critically. 'You're not that old. You must be…what…five years younger than my dad?'

'Ten years younger, to be exact,' Kate said dryly, 'but it's a sad fact of life that a man in his thirties is considered to be in his prime, whereas a woman heading that way is practically over the hill.'

'My dad wouldn't ever want to get married again, no matter how old he was,' Jodie observed as she followed Kate along to her father's study. 'He loved my mother too much.'

'Of course he did,' Kate said softly, seeing the pride and love in the girl's face. 'OK, that's us,' she added, propping the note on Ethan's desk. 'Martin will see it when he gets back and he can tell the others where we've gone.'

But as she cheerfully banged the study door shut behind them, the piece of paper fluttered gently off the desk and landed unobtrusively in the waste-paper basket.

'The BMW's still in the garage, sir, and none of the bicycles are missing,' Ted Burton said, his normally cheery face creased with worry.

'What about a bus? Does any bus go past the entrance to Malden?'

Ted gazed at Rhona who was twisting her apron convulsively between her fingers.

'The only bus which goes past Malden is the half past nine one in the morning to Hexham, Dr Flett,' she said, her voice distinctly shaky. 'And Kate and Jodie were both still here then.'

'Any news, Martin?' Ethan continued, whirling on his heel as his secretary appeared in the hall.

'Nothing. I've checked all the hospitals within a fifty-mile radius and none of them has admitted anyone answering to Jodie's or Kate's description.'

'Then where the hell are they?' Ethan demanded, his face white and strained. 'They can't just have vanished into thin air.'

'Shall I check the grounds again, Dr Flett?' Ted asked. 'Maybe if I went further this time—right to the outskirts of the estate?'

'They'd hardly walk that far in this weather,' Ethan retorted. 'Rhona, you're absolutely certain the house looked undisturbed when you got back? There was no sign of a struggle, no indication of a forced entry?'

'Everything was completely in order, Dr Flett,' she said tearfully. 'I just wish I'd stayed home. If I'd stayed home...'

Her voice trailed away into silence and Ethan paced the hall restlessly. Call the police, his mind urged, you have to call the police—but calling the police meant accepting the unthinkable, that his daughter might have been kidnapped, and he didn't even want to consider that, far less think it.

'I'll go out in the car again,' he said at last. 'Maybe I didn't drive far enough last time. Martin, you stay by the phone in case someone should ring, Ted...' He paused and shook his head. 'Try the grounds again—maybe Jodie fell, hurt herself.'

Nobody said the obvious—that if Jodie had fallen why hadn't Kate come back to the house for help?

'Call me on my mobile if you hear anything,' Ethan continued as he walked quickly out of the house, with Rhona and Ted having almost to run to keep up with him. 'Any information you receive, no matter how small or trivial—'

He came to a halt. Faintly but clearly they could all hear the sound of feminine laughter.

'She's all right,' Rhona breathed as two distinctly dishevelled figures suddenly emerged from the woods near the house. 'Praise be to God, the wee lassie's all right.'

Jodie was clearly a lot better than just all right, Ethan thought as he watched his daughter dancing towards them. He hadn't seen her looking so relaxed and happy for years, and although relief flooded through him it was a relief which was almost immediately superseded by anger.

It wasn't Jodie's fault, he told himself, clenching his fists tight against his thighs until his knuckles showed white.

She was just a child, with a child's natural impetuosity, but Kate...

Oh, he could blame her all right, he thought, trying hard to ignore the way her damp T-shirt was outlining a pair of unexpectedly full breasts and her ancient shorts were revealing a pair of dirt-smudged legs that shouldn't have been even remotely sexy and yet somehow were. She had put him through hell for the last hour and a half, and she had no right to appear so unconcerned or to possess the ability to jolt his body into such rampant awareness at the sight of her.

'Oh, Dad, we've had such a great time,' Jodie cried, throwing her arms round his neck in greeting. 'Kate and I went down to the river and—'

'I think you'd better go upstairs and get changed,' he declared, his voice tight.

'In a minute,' she said excitedly. 'There was this fisherman down by the river, and he had a heart attack right in front of our eyes. Kate did that CRP thing—'

'CPR,' he corrected automatically. 'Cardiopulmonary resuscitation.'

'That's right.' She nodded. 'I did the breathing while Kate pressed on his chest to get his heart started again, and the ambulanceman said I did really well for a beginner, and—'

'And right now I'd like you to get out of those damp clothes,' Ethan interrupted.

A puzzled frown creased his daughter's forehead. 'Are you angry with me, Dad?'

'Of course I'm not,' he replied, his smile forced, 'but Rhona will be serving your tea soon and you know what she's like if you're late. You can tell me about the fisherman after tea,' he continued as his daughter opened her mouth, clearly intending to protest, 'but right now I want you to scoot. No, not you, Kate,' he added as she made to follow Jodie. 'You I want to talk to.'

His voice was quiet, ominously so, and Kate glanced up at him quickly.

'What's happened?' she asked.

'Not here—my study,' he replied, his voice clipped, turning on his heel.

A cold chill ran down her back. He looked so white, so drained, and unwillingly she found herself remembering that the fisherman's driving licence had said he was only three years older than Ethan. Had Bill Torrance's prediction come all too horribly true and he'd been taken ill while he was in Newcastle?

Swiftly she followed him along to his study, and as soon as they reached it she caught hold of his arm with concern.

'What is it—what's wrong?'

'You have the gall to ask me that?' he asked bitingly, throwing off her hand. 'Do you really think for one minute that I enjoy coming home after an exhausting day in Newcastle to find my daughter missing and the entire household in an uproar because the nurse I employ is either too lazy or too damn stupid to think of leaving a note to tell us where she's going?'

'B-but I did leave a note,' she stammered. 'I would never—'

'Have you no sense of responsibility?' he thundered, his eyes blazing. 'Didn't it even cross your mind once that we might be worried sick?'

'Ethan, I left a note,' she insisted.

Disbelief was clear on his face and she pushed past him to stare in bewilderment at the empty desk.

'I put it there,' she muttered in confusion. 'I put it down there.'

'Oh, for heaven's sake, don't lie,' he said derisively as she circled his desk, her eyes fixed on the floor. 'If there's one thing I hate more than inefficiency, it's someone lying to me.'

'Here—here it is!' she exclaimed, retrieving the sheet of

paper, her face triumphant. 'It must have blown into the waste-paper basket when I shut the door.'

Ethan stared down at the note, then at Kate. It vindicated her completely and he should have felt pleased, but instead he felt extremely foolish—and it was a condition he was both unfamiliar with and discovered he didn't like.

'OK', he said grimly, reaching into his desk. 'As you appear to be in an explaining mood today, perhaps you'd care to explain these.'

He threw a collection of brochures down onto the desk in front of her and Kate's heart sank. They were all from design colleges. Jodie must have been writing to them to ask for details of the courses they offered.

'Where did you get them?' she asked quietly.

'I thought it was strange when all these large envelopes kept coming in addressed to Jodie—'

'You *opened* your daughter's mail?' she gasped.

A faint tinge of colour appeared on his cheeks. 'It is my duty to ensure she doesn't do anything which might endanger her health.'

'And that duty extends to opening her post, does it?' she said, her voice as tight as his.

'She is my child—'

'Ethan, she isn't a child,' she protested. 'She's almost fifteen and she wants to go to design college. You have to let her go. She's so talented—'

'How the hell can she go to college?' he demanded impatiently, sitting down behind his desk. 'You know her condition—she'd never be able to cope.'

'She would. She's already doing quite a bit of her own physio—'

'She's doing *what*?'

His voice was like a whiplash and Kate flushed scarlet, but it was too late to take back what she'd said, and he'd been bound to find out eventually.

'She's not in any danger,' she said as calmly as she could. 'I'm keeping an eye on her—'

'You are not paid to keep an eye on her,' he roared. 'You are paid to do your job as laid down in your contract. Any deviation from that—*any* deviation—has to be agreed by me.'

'Jodie has rights, too,' she muttered rebelliously under her breath, but he heard her.

'Who the hell do you think you are?' he exploded. 'You waltz in here, thinking that because you've read a few books you know all there is to know about the condition, but this is my daughter we're talking about!'

'I understand—'

'You don't,' he interrupted, his lips a thin white line of anger. 'All the book-learning in the world can never make you understand what it's like to look at someone you love and know they might not be alive next week or next month.'

'Ethan—'

'No amount of nursing experience can make you understand how it feels to watch someone you love suffer,' he continued, his blue eyes hard. 'So until you've personally done that, until you've personally endured that, you know nothing, lady!'

But I do know, she thought, as unwelcome memories stirred in her mind—memories of the stench of blood mixed with stale urine, memories of a man thrashing about in agony. I do know, and I wish to God I didn't.

'Ethan, please…please, stop,' she begged, but he didn't.

'Ignorant'…'irresponsible'…'feckless'. Dimly she could hear his accusations but all she was aware of was that somehow she had to make him stop. Somehow she had to silence that voice which was making her feel sick and giddy as memories flooded into her mind of things she didn't want to remember, of a time she had tried so hard to forget—and she did the only thing she could think of. She reached for the vase of flowers on his desk and emptied the entire contents over his head.

'Shut up!' she cried, as he leapt to his feet, spluttering and coughing. 'Just, please…please, shut up! My husband died of leukaemia two years ago and I nursed him at home for the last year of his life. For a whole year I listened to him fighting and choking for breath. For a whole year I watched him die little by little, day after day, so don't you dare…don't you *dare* tell me I don't understand!'

He didn't say anything. He was too busy wiping water from his face and pulling bits of flowers off his jacket, and as her anger and grief subsided she gazed at him in horror.

'Ethan, I'm sorry… I shouldn't…I didn't…'

His head came up, shock plain on his face, and she gave one ragged cry and fled—and didn't stop running until she'd reached the safety of her rooms.

How could she have done that, how *could* she? she wondered as she slumped down on her bed. In all her years of nursing she'd never lost control, and to assault a patient's father…!

A shuddering sob escaped her as she reached under the bed and dragged out her suitcase. There was no point in postponing the inevitable. He'd sack her for sure and it was better to leave voluntarily than be thrown out. However, she'd scarcely opened her case when she heard a knock on her sitting-room door.

For a second she considered ignoring it, but she knew she couldn't. Jodie might be ill, and no matter how wretched she personally felt, the needs of her patient were still paramount.

But it wasn't Jodie who was standing outside in the corridor. It was Ethan.

Droplets of water were still running down from his hair onto his wet suit, and bits of leaves and petals were sticking at jaunty angles to his jacket. At any other time she might have found his appearance funny but right then she didn't feel like laughing.

'It's OK—I'm going,' she muttered as she went back into the bedroom. 'You didn't have to come in person to throw me out.'

'Kate—'

'If I could just have fifteen minutes to pack—'

'Kate, I'm not sacking you.'

She looked round at him in amazement. 'But you can't want me to stay, not after…not after…'

'You gave me an impromptu shower?'

She gazed at him, open-mouthed. He'd made a joke. She'd just behaved unforgivably, and he'd made a joke.

'Ethan—'

'Why didn't you tell me about your husband?' he demanded, all amusement gone from his face.

She shook her head blindly. 'There was no need for you to know. You're my boss…you…I…' She came to a halt and to her horror tears began to trickle down her cheeks, tears that became great gulping sobs, and before she could do anything about them she was in his arms and he was cradling her head on his shoulder.

'I'm sorry…I'm so sorry,' she gasped into his chest. 'Crying like this… I'm sorry…'

'I'm the one who should be doing the apologising,' he said fiercely, holding her tighter. 'I'm the one who just behaved with all the sensitivity of a flea.'

A hiccuping laugh broke from her. 'It wasn't your fault. You weren't to know—'

'That's no excuse,' he interrupted. 'Kate…oh, Kate, don't ever apologise for being upset. Don't ever apologise for feeling.'

His voice was so gentle, so full of remorse, that her tears began afresh and she dashed a shaking hand across them. 'I'm sorry—'

'What did I just say?' he demanded, gripping her hands firmly.

'Never apologise for crying,' she said with a watery smile. 'Never say you're sorry. Is…is it OK to ask to borrow a handkerchief?'

He chuckled but to her surprise he didn't give her the handkerchief. Instead, he used it himself to carefully wipe away her tears.

'Kate…'

'Yes?' she said shakily, her tears still far too near the surface for comfort.

'Kate.'

To her strained senses his voice sounded different— deeper, a little husky. Don't be silly, she told herself. He's being kind, sympathetic, as any good boss should be.

'Yes?' she said again, this time more firmly.

He didn't say anything. He simply reached out and, oh, so gently, smoothed her damp hair back from her forehead. For a second she didn't move, scarcely dared to breathe, but when his fingers left her hair and cupped her chin she couldn't help herself. Involuntarily she stiffened, and he released her abruptly.

'Do you have a passport?'

'A what?' she asked, blinking both at his bizarre question and the sudden harshness of his tone.

'A passport—do you have a valid passport?'

'No, I've never—'

'I have friends in the Home Office so it shouldn't take more than a day or two.'

'But I don't need a passport,' she exclaimed. 'I'm not going anywhere.'

'You are—we all are. Bill said this morning that this weather was bad for Jodie, and you told me I needed a holiday, so we're going to Austria.'

She pressed her fingertips to her forehead and wondered whether she was going mad or if he was.

'Ethan, we can't just go to Austria,' she protested. 'Jodie can't just *go* anywhere. We'd have to inform the airline authority that she'd be carrying a compressor and oxygen cylinders, and we'll never be able to get a hotel booking at such short notice. And then there's your deadline—'

'Martin can see to the airline authority, we don't need a hotel because I own a chalet near Kitzbühel, and I've got an extension to my deadline. Kate, we need a holiday,' he continued as she stared at him in amazement. 'Rhona included.'

'She's coming with us?' she said faintly.

'Of course she is. There's no way I'm living without her home cooking for the next three or four weeks. Now, put that suitcase away and tomorrow get yourself across to Alnwick and have some passport photos taken.'

He'd got as far as the door before she pulled her scattered wits together.

'Ethan, why are you doing this?' she asked. 'You should be sacking me for what I did, not taking me to Austria.'

A half-smile appeared on his lips. 'My sister would probably say I had it coming.'

'Ethan, I'm being serious,' she protested, her brown eyes large and troubled. 'Why?'

For a second he said nothing, then he smiled again, this time a little crookedly. 'Let's just say I think we could all do with a break. Myself included.'

Which is why I must be completely out of my mind to suggest we go to Kitzbühel, he thought with a groan as he went out of the door.

He'd never intended suggesting it—he didn't even know now where the idea had come from. All he'd known was that she'd been upset, he'd been responsible, and he'd wanted to make her happy. What hadn't occurred to him until she'd gazed up at him with those big spaniel eyes of hers had been that if he couldn't control his intrusive libido in a house as large as Malden what hope did he have of controlling it in a four-bedroom chalet?

He would just have to control it, he told himself firmly. Having made the suggestion to go there, he couldn't possibly renege on it now, and at least Austria had one thing in its favour. It boasted mile upon mile of exhausting and exacting walks. Which was just as well really, he thought ruefully as he made his way down the corridor, because he had the horribly depressing feeling he was going to need them.

CHAPTER FOUR

'It's beautiful—so beautiful,' Kate breathed as she leaned over the veranda railing and stared out at the flower-filled meadow and the Kitzbüheler Alps beyond. 'The painted houses, the mountains, the cows with the bells round their necks—it's like every photograph I've ever seen.'

'So you keep saying.' Jodie chuckled. 'In fact, you've said nothing else since we got here.'

'Sorry.' Kate laughed. 'It's just…well, everything's so perfect.'

'Have you seen my dad this morning?'

Well, perhaps not quite perfect, Kate thought with a sigh, turning reluctantly away from the stunning view.

She hadn't seen Ethan. In fact, since they'd arrived in Austria three days ago she'd scarcely seen him at all, even for meals. If he wasn't closeted with his agent, discussing essential repairs and maintenance to the chalet, he was out, having apparently—and somewhat surprisingly—developed a sudden taste for hiking.

Of course, she was pleased by his absence. It meant he was finally allowing Jodie some independence. It meant he trusted her to look after his daughter. And it also meant she'd been given the time to get the disturbing feelings she'd experienced back at Malden into perspective and recognise them for what they were—the inevitable result of living in too close proximity to a very attractive man.

So it would have been singularly ridiculous and perverse of her if she'd found herself missing him. Of course it would, she told herself with another sigh.

'He's probably seeing Mr Roscher again,' she murmured. 'Or maybe he's gone out for another walk.'

'He can't have,' Jodie protested. 'I told him last night that Rhona was having lunch with that British couple who are staying in the chalet down the road so he'd have to drive us to Kitzbühel.'

'Maybe he's forgotten.'

'My dad never forgets. Mind you...' the girl giggled '...he was never a fitness fanatic before either. Oh, well, you'll just have to drive us.'

'Me?' Kate said faintly.

Jodie nodded. 'It's a pity he's not around because he would have been company for you while I was having my tennis lesson.'

Darn the company, Kate thought with a sinking heart. What I want is a driver—any driver. Ethan's chalet might be only ten miles from the town, but it was ten miles of the most spectacular hairpin bends she'd ever seen—hairpin bends that had her sitting white-knuckled as a passenger next to Rhona, so heaven alone knew what it would be like to drive herself.

'Look, I know my dad can be a bit of a pain at times,' Jodie declared, clearly misinterpreting her silence, 'but he's not a bad old stick, and you quite like him, don't you?'

She did. She liked him a lot. He drove her nuts at times, of course, with his assumption that he was always right, but, then, nobody was perfect. Even Simon hadn't been able to hide his impatience with her shyness, she remembered. And he'd hated the way she could never refuse anyone a favour, and...

And what in the world was she doing? She was actually criticising Simon. She was actually comparing him to Ethan, but Simon had been her husband, and she'd loved him, whereas Ethan...

'You haven't answered my question,' Jodie pressed, her blue eyes suddenly troubled. 'My dad—you do like him, don't you?'

With difficulty Kate pulled herself back to the present.

'I'd like any man who brought me to a place as beautiful as this,' she said briskly. 'Now, do you know if Rhona wants us to get her anything from the shops when we're in town?' she added, determinedly changing the subject.

'Just some indigestion tablets from the chemist.'

A frown pleated Kate's forehead. She distinctly remembered Rhona buying a packet when they'd first arrived—and she needed more already? Unconsciously she shook her head. She was going to have to talk to Ethan about Rhona's health, promise or no promise.

'Ready to go down to Kitzbühel?'

'Dad!' Jodie exclaimed with delight, turning to see him standing in the doorway to the veranda. 'I thought you'd forgotten about me.'

'Fat chance after all those reminders last night.' He grinned. 'All set to leave, Kate?'

Was it her imagination or did he look distinctly uncomfortable when he turned to her? His grin had certainly disappeared, and when Jodie dashed away to collect her tennis bag he didn't even attempt to make any conversation but simply stood, drumming his fingers on the veranda rail, as though anxious to be gone.

Of course he was anxious to be gone, she thought. Being stuck with your daughter's nurse for a whole morning couldn't be the most scintillating prospect in the world, and the very least she could do was tell him she was grateful.

'I really am pleased you're coming with us this morning,' she said quickly.

She might have been mistaken about him looking uncomfortable, but there was no mistaking the surprise in his face as he turned towards her. 'Are you?'

'And how.' She nodded fervently. 'The thought of driving that road…!'

'The road?'

'You can call me chicken if you want,' she said with a laugh, 'but all those twists and bends terrify me rigid.'

'Ah.'

There was an odd look of disappointment in his eyes and she couldn't think why. She'd have thought he'd have preferred her to be honest about her driving limitations rather than profess a skill she didn't have.

'Ethan—'

'All ready, Dad!' Jodie cried, bouncing back onto the veranda, clutching her tennis bag.

'Let's go, then,' he replied abruptly.

And without waiting for a reply he led the way out to his car, leaving Kate with the very distinct impression that she had managed to hurt him—but she couldn't for the life of her think how.

To her relief whatever had bothered him seemed to have disappeared by the time they reached Kitzbühel, and he appeared genuinely pleased when he discovered Jodie's lesson wasn't until eleven o'clock.

'We've an hour to kill, then,' he observed. 'Does anyone have any suggestions on how we fill it?'

When Rhona drove them down she normally left Kate to explore the old walled town with its quaintly cobbled streets, stone stairways and picturesque medieval buildings, while she disappeared into one of the many cafés to enjoy a cup of coffee and some gateau, but deliberately Kate said nothing, waiting to see what the others would suggest.

'What would you like to do, Kate?' Ethan asked, turning to her unexpectedly.

'The Pfaffkirche—the local parish church—sounds interesting,' she said tentatively. 'According to the guide book the paintings on the ceilings are truly amazing. Or there's the Liebfrauenkirche—the Church of our Lady?' she continued quickly, seeing Jodie's eyes roll heavenwards. 'Apparently it used to be an important place of pilgrimage.'

'What about the local museum?' Ethan suggested. 'I seem to recall it had a marvellous model of a silver mine.'

'Wow,' Jodie muttered expressively. 'A church or a museum—I can hardly wait.'

A gurgle of laughter came from Kate. 'I think maybe we should just get ourselves something to drink.'

'Sounds fine to me,' Jodie declared with ill-disguised relief. 'Just give me a minute to buy Aunt Di a postcard and I'll be right with you.'

Ethan shook his head ruefully as Jodie ran across the road to the Tabak. 'My daughter isn't exactly subtle about her likes and dislikes, is she?'

'I keep telling you, she's a teenager.' Kate smiled. 'Stroppiness is written into their contract.'

He laughed, then a slight frown creased his forehead. 'Who's that she's talking to?'

Kate followed the direction of his gaze. Jodie was deep in laughing conversation with a group of young people she recognised as members of the tennis club.

'Just some friends she's made,' she answered.

Ethan looked as though he wanted to say more but he didn't get the chance to. Jodie came flying back to them, her face excited.

'Dad, my friends are going for a walk down by the river. Can I go with them?'

'But what about your tennis lesson?' he protested.

'Franz has a lesson at eleven o'clock, too, so he'll make sure I'm back in time. Can I go, Dad, please?'

All of Ethan's protective instincts told him to refuse but as he stared at his daughter's eager face he suddenly noticed something else. Kate was mouthing the words, 'Let her go.' To his surprise he found himself nodding.

'OK, but don't forget to take your enzyme capsules if you eat anything, and if you find yourself getting the least bit sweaty—'

'Take some salt tablets,' Jodie interrupted as Kate handed them to her. 'I know, Dad.'

'And watch you don't walk too far—'

'*Dad!*'

'OK, OK.' He smiled wryly. 'We'll be leaving Kitzbühel at twelve-thirty so I want you back here at the car by twelve twenty-five. And don't worry about us,' he added, unnecessarily, for in truth his daughter didn't look in the least bit concerned. 'We'll fill in the time looking for a birthday present for you.'

The smile on Jodie's face became distinctly fixed, and as her father went to the car to retrieve her tennis bag she grasped Kate's arm quickly.

'Don't let him out of your sight for a second, and don't let him buy me anything to wear,' she entreated. 'Make him buy me a watch or a necklace.'

'But you really could do with some new clothes,' Kate protested. 'All I've ever seen you wearing is that jogging suit, or a pair of jeans and a sweatshirt.'

'If you'd seen the rest of the things in my wardrobe you'd know why!' Jodie wailed. 'Dad buys all my clothes and he buys the kind of thing a five-year-old wouldn't be seen dead in!'

Kate shook her head and laughed. 'Oh, come on, Jodie, stop exaggerating.'

'It's true,' the girl declared vehemently. 'If you don't stop him he'll buy me some awful velvet dress with a big white collar, or some dorky party dress in pink chiffon with a bow. Make him buy me some jewellery,' she muttered as Ethan walked towards them. 'I'll never forgive you if you don't!'

Kate wanted to ask just how she was supposed to dissuade Ethan from doing something he'd really set his mind on but she was too late. He had already joined them.

'Have you enough money, sweetheart?' he asked, reaching into his pocket.

'Plenty,' she replied, edging away, clearly anxious to be gone.

'Enjoy yourself, then,' he said, trying—and failing—to smile.

She didn't even reply. She was already halfway across the road and Ethan watched her until she disappeared from sight.

'I know, I know,' he said ruefully as he turned to find Kate's gaze on him. 'I worry too much.'

'They're good kids, Ethan,' she said softly. 'They know all about Jodie's CF and they've accepted it, and that's what she needs. To feel part of the crowd.'

'I guess so,' he replied, leading the way down a side street and then into the Vorderstadt, one of Kitzbühel's pedestrian precincts. 'I'm just surprised she's become so keen on tennis all of a sudden. Back at Malden you practically had to drag her onto the court.'

'Ah, but back at Malden we didn't have Franz Zimmerman.' Kate chuckled.

'Franz Zimmerman?'

'The eighteen-year-old son of one of the local hoteliers who happens to be blond, blue-eyed and drop-dead gorgeous.'

He stopped dead in the middle of the pavement and shot her a penetrating glance. 'Is he indeed?'

Kate shook her head and chuckled again. 'Jodie will come to no harm with him, I can assure you. He's a nice boy.'

'I'm sure he is, but it's not unheard of for nice boys to get nice girls into trouble.'

'And it's not unheard of for nice fathers to have coronaries, worrying needlessly about the things that might happen to their daughters,' she said firmly. 'Now, about this birthday present for her—'

'Later,' he interrupted, taking her by the elbow and steering her firmly towards one of the pavement cafés. 'Right now what I want is a really good cup of coffee.'

She couldn't disagree with that. A really good cup of

coffee sounded wonderful, and as he settled her in a seat and beckoned to a hovering waiter she sat back and admired the view.

And what a view. All the buildings opposite had been painted in bright blues and pinks and yellows, and she supposed it should have looked awful but it didn't. In fact, there was nothing about this town she didn't like. She loved the quaint houses, the postcard-perfect costumes of the locals, and even her inability to speak the language didn't detract from her enjoyment but merely added to the charm.

'Sorry—did you say something?' she faltered, suddenly aware that Ethan was gazing at her expectantly.

'You're miles away, aren't you?' He laughed. 'What are you thinking about?'

'This,' she said happily, waving her hands towards the painted murals on the buildings and the Alps towering above the town. 'It's like being on a film set but it's not a film set, it's real, and I'm actually here.'

'You should have come abroad before.'

'Simon and I always intended to travel, but...' Her voice trailed away into silence. Ethan waited until the waiter had brought their coffees before saying, 'Tell me about him, Kate.'

She gazed at him in surprise. 'Tell you what?'

'Everything. What he was like, what he did for a living, how long you were married...'

'I have a photograph of him,' she began, reaching into her bag, only to pause and colour faintly. 'Sorry—there's no need for you to—'

'What did I tell you before about apologising?' he interrupted, his eyebrows raised quizzically.

'Sorry. Oh, heck, I didn't mean to say that,' she said, beginning to laugh as he groaned. 'I meant...I meant...'

'Just give me the photograph, woman.' He grinned, taking it from her. He stared at it for a moment, then handed it back. 'Looks a nice bloke.'

Her lips curved into a gentle smile. 'He was. We met at the Birnham Infirmary when we were both student nurses, and I guess…I guess you could say it was a case of love at first sight. We didn't get married until I was twenty-two. We wanted to finish our training first.'

'So you were married for five years?'

She stared at him in amazement and he smiled a little ruefully. 'You said in your CV that you were twenty-nine, and you told me Simon died two years ago so it didn't take much calculation to work it out.'

No, it didn't, but what surprised her was that he had been interested enough to do it.

'You said he died of leukaemia?' he continued, taking a sip of his coffee.

'Chronic myeloid leukaemia, to be exact.'

He frowned. 'That's pretty unusual for a man of what…twenty-six?'

'Twenty-seven.' Her brown eyes darkened slightly. 'He was always complaining about being tired and I used to get so angry, thinking he was simply making up excuses to avoid doing things around the house.'

'When did you realise something was wrong?' he asked gently.

'I didn't,' she said harshly. 'Oh, I knew he'd been losing weight, but he'd always been a bit vain about his figure—going to the gym, exercising regularly. It was the number of chest infections he kept getting that made me nag him into seeing our doctor.'

'And that's when the chronic myeloid leukaemia was diagnosed?'

She nodded. 'They tried everything. Anti-cancer drugs, immunoglobulin injections to boost his immune system, radiotherapy. The one real hope was a bone-marrow transplant but they couldn't find a match.'

'Kate, you have to stop feeling guilty,' he said softly, his blue eyes seeing what nobody else ever had. 'You couldn't possibly have diagnosed what was wrong. The symptoms are so vague at the beginning—tiredness, sweating a lot at night, weight loss.'

'But I'm a nurse,' she replied wretchedly. 'If I'd paid more attention—'

'He was a nurse, too, remember,' he pointed out.

'Yes, but men always stick their heads in the sand when it comes to illness,' she retorted. 'If I'd done more, instead of just getting irritated with him, he might have lived.'

'You don't know that,' he insisted. 'Nobody does, and he was a grown man, Kate. His health was his responsibility, not yours.'

'Perhaps,' she murmured. 'And now—if you don't mind—I'd rather not talk about it any more,' she said as he opened his mouth, clearly intending to do just that. 'You're supposed to be on holiday and I'm sure the last thing you want to do is talk about my past.'

He wanted to tell her she was wrong, that he longed to know everything about her. He wanted to tell her he found her beautiful and desirable but he knew she'd run a mile if he did. That or slap his face, and from the wary looks he'd caught her giving him lately he rather thought it would be the latter.

'Kate…'

She wasn't even looking at him, far less listening.

'What is it—what's wrong?' he asked, glancing over his shoulder to see what had attracted her attention.

'That little boy at the table by the tree,' she said with concern. 'I don't like the look of— Oh, my God!'

Ethan was out of his seat and running at the same moment she was, sending the tray of cups in the hands of the unlucky waiter who had been passing behind him crashing to the ground.

They reached the child together and without a word of explanation Ethan pulled the boy from his distraught mother's arms and laid him flat on the ground.

It was clear even to the uninitiated that the child was choking. His face was blue, his eyes were rolling. Swiftly Ethan placed his two hands one on top of the other between the child's navel and ribcage and pressed down with a quick, upward thrust.

'It's not shifting,' he muttered as he tried the procedure again, and then again. 'Whatever is stuck in his trachea isn't shifting. Kate, I need a sharp knife and some kind of tubing.'

He can't be serious, she thought. He can't honestly be intending to carry out a tracheotomy in the middle of a crowded pavement café. But one look at his taut face told her it was the child's only chance.

Quickly she grabbed a steak knife and a plastic ballpoint pen from one of the tables near to them. 'Are these any use?'

He didn't even answer. He simply dismantled the pen, doused it and the knife with a bottle of mineral water, and without hesitation made a swift incision into the child's neck and inserted the pen barrel into his trachea to create a makeshift endotracheal tube.

The effect was miraculous. Within seconds the child's breathing became easier and a faint tinge of pink appeared on his cheeks.

'I hope somebody's phoned for an ambulance,' Ethan murmured as a collective sigh of relief ran round the on-lookers and a woman began to cry. 'I've bought him time, but that pen isn't going to work indefinitely.'

It didn't need to. The wail of a fast-approaching ambulance suddenly rent the air, and within minutes the boy and his tearful mother were being whisked away to hospital.

'That has to be the most amazing piece of surgery I've ever seen,' Kate declared in admiration as they returned to their table after Ethan had shrugged off the congratulations of the bystanders with clear embarrassment.

'You'd have done the same. You would, Kate,' he said

as she began to shake her head. 'If it was either do what I did or watch the boy die, you'd have done it, too.'

He was right and she chuckled. 'OK, but all I can say is if that's an example of what you can achieve with a steak knife and a pen, I'd love to see what you can do in a fully equipped operating theatre.'

He stared at her for a moment, then his lips curved wryly. 'My sister's been talking to you, hasn't she?'

'No,' she began, only to flush slightly as his eyebrows rose. 'OK, yes, she has, but what I said—I didn't say it because I was trying to persuade you to go back to work.'

'You couldn't if you tried,' he said.

'Ethan—'

'It's half past eleven,' he continued, getting to his feet. 'I'd better see what I can find for Jodie's birthday next week or she'll be back before we know it.'

'Have you any idea what you're going to buy?' she asked absently, vexed that he should imagine her praise had possessed an ulterior motive when her response had been solely motivated by admiration of his skill.

'I thought a dress. Something she could wear for going out in the evening when we get back to Malden.'

Kate forbore from pointing out that as his daughter rarely went out in daylight back at Malden, far less in the evening, it seemed a somewhat pointless gift.

'Jewellery's always very acceptable,' she said, remembering Jodie's impassioned plea. 'What about a watch or a necklace?'

He shook his head. 'I think I'll stick with the dress. There's a shop over there that looks as though it might have what I'm looking for. Have another cup of coffee—I won't be long.'

She stared at him uncertainly. Don't let him out of your sight for a second, Jodie had said. Well, she hadn't managed to dissuade him from buying the girl clothes so she supposed she ought to fulfil at least one part of her instruction.

'I'll come with you,' she said, getting to her feet.

'There's no need—'

'Of course there isn't.' She smiled. 'But sometimes two heads are better than one when it comes to choosing a present.'

He shrugged, and as Kate followed him across the road and into the shop her spirits rose. Jodie might have insisted she didn't want her father to buy her anything to wear, but she couldn't see how the girl could object to anything bought from such a stylish establishment.

'Morgen! Wie kann ich Ihnen hilfen?' the shopkeeper said with a beaming smile as soon as she saw her.

Kate smiled back apologetically. 'I'm sorry, but do you speak English at all?'

'Ja, of course.' The woman nodded. 'How can I help?'

'We're looking for a dress. Something a soon-to-be fifteen-year-old would like to wear for going out in the evening.'

'Something stylish but not too modern?' the woman suggested. 'Something that will make her feel grown up, but not make her look too old for her years?'

'Exactly,' Kate replied with relief. 'I thought perhaps—'

'What about this, Kate?' Ethan asked. 'This is pretty.'

Kate turned to see what he had found and had difficulty crushing down her laughter. It was a blue velvet dress with a large white collar.

'You're in the children's section, Ethan.'

'It's a lovely dress.'

'It would be if Jodie was ten but she's not.'

'Then what about this?' he said, lifting down a pink, frothy confection with a large red bow at the waist.

She shook her head firmly and quickly flicked through one of the rails beside her.

'Now, this,' she declared, pulling out a short, body-hugging dress in black satin, 'this is more like the thing.'

'But it's a petticoat,' he protested.

'It's a dress, Ethan,' she replied witheringly.

'Well, it doesn't look like one,' he muttered. 'And the colour—surely she'll never want to wear black?'

'She'll love it—trust me.'

'It looks like I'm going to have to,' he said, sounding distinctly aggrieved. 'Is there anything else you'd think she'd just love while we're here?'

There was no mistaking the sarcasm in his voice but she smiled at him sweetly.

'She could do with some blouses and a couple of pairs of trousers, if you're serious?'

He shrugged and, taking that for agreement, she quickly flicked through the rail again and selected two brightly coloured overshirts and some dazzling trousers.

'How about these?' she asked, holding them up for him to see.

He rolled his eyes. 'Wonderful. She can look like a clown by day and a widow at night. Maybe you'd like me to get her this, too?' he added, lifting up a cream leather bomber jacket.

'Oh, that is beautiful,' she said in delight. 'She'll love that.'

'Have you seen the price?' he exclaimed.

She hadn't, but she scowled at him nevertheless. 'Oh, for heaven's sake, don't be such a skinflint. Your daughter's birthday only comes round once a year.'

'Just as well,' he said with feeling. 'OK, we'll take that, too.'

The shopkeeper chuckled as Kate handed the garments to her. 'Always the men they do not understand the price of fashion. *Seiner mann* is no different to all the rest.'

'*Seiner mann*?' Kate repeated with a frown.

'*Ja*, your husband.'

Hot colour flew into Kate's cheeks. 'But he's not my husband. I'm his nurse. I mean I'm his daughter's nurse,' she floundered, reddening still further.

'Ah,' the shopkeeper declared with a knowing wink that left Kate in no doubt whatsoever as to what kind of relationship she believed she enjoyed with Ethan.

Red-cheeked with embarrassment, Kate waited only until Ethan had written a cheque and carried the parcels along to his car, before rounding on him.

'Why didn't you say something?' she protested as he opened the boot. 'That woman thinks...she thinks you and I...'

'I know.' He grinned. 'Kate, people believe what they want to believe,' he said as she opened her mouth angrily. 'And, believe me, she'd never accept that anybody but a wife or a mistress could browbeat a man into spending so much money.'

'So much money?' A momentary qualm assailed her. 'Ethan, how...how much did you just spend?'

He told her.

'*What?*' she gasped. 'Oh, Ethan, take some of the clothes back. Tell that woman I made a mistake and we only want the dress!'

He caught her by the shoulders and whirled her round, his face alight with laughter. 'Kate, you are priceless! First you accuse me of being a skinflint, and then you insist I take most of it back. You are adorable!'

And, as if to prove it, he kissed her.

It all happened too quickly, that was the trouble. One minute his lips were gentle, feather-light, the lips of a friend, and the next they were urgent, demanding, so that even before she had time to think her own lips had parted helplessly beneath his.

Nobody had ever kissed her like that. Nobody—not even Simon—had made her body feel as though it were dissolving, melting, in a warm sea of sensation. Dimly she heard him groan but as her arms snaked of their own accord round his neck all she was aware of was the desire to have him closer, the need to feel his lean, hard strength pressed against her.

It was that need which suddenly made her aware of his own patent arousal. It was that need which acted like a dousing with icy water, bringing home to her the enormity of what she was doing. With a muffled cry she dragged herself out of his arms, her cheeks scarlet, her heart pounding.

'Kate, I'm sorry,' he said hoarsely, knowing he was anything but. 'Kate, don't look at me like that, so stricken, so—'

'Twenty-five past twelve on the dot!'

They turned in unison to see Jodie running down the street, and Kate knew she had never been so relieved to see anyone in her life.

'Did you have a good time, sweetheart?' Ethan asked brightly, too brightly.

'Fantastic.' She beamed. 'We walked almost halfway round the lake and then went to the tennis courts. Herr Zimmerman asked for you, Kate. He wanted to know where my pretty nurse was.'

'Herr Zimmerman?' Ethan repeated, his dark eyebrows snapping down.

'Franz's father—I told you about him,' Kate murmured, totally unable to meet his eyes. 'And now it's time we got you home, young lady,' she went on. 'You've got your physio to do before lunch, remember?'

Jodie nodded and got into the car, and if both Kate and her father seemed to answer most of her comments in mono syllables on the way home she didn't seem to notice.

'Did you persuade him to buy me jewellery?' she whispered when they drew up outside the house.

Kate shook her head. 'I didn't, but you'll love the clothes he bought you, I promise.'

Jodie went into the house with distinctly dragging steps, looking anything but convinced, but as Kate made to follow her Ethan blocked her path.

'Kate, I need to talk to you.'

'Later,' she replied, trying to sidestep him without success. 'Jodie's physio—'

'Can wait ten minutes. Kate…' He reached out and touched her cheek and to his dismay saw her flinch. 'Kate, I apologised for what I did down in Kitzbühel but I was wrong. I'm not one bit sorry for kissing you, and I don't think you are if you'd be honest with yourself.'

'How can you say that?' she flared. 'You don't know what I think, what I feel!'

'No, but I do know you enjoyed that kiss every bit as much as I did until you began to feel guilty,' he replied.

She shook her head vehemently. 'You're wrong—wrong!'

He caught hold of her hand and refused to let go.

'Kate, you didn't die with Simon. Life goes on, and it's right that it should, just as it's right that the memories of loved ones become less sharp along with the pain.'

It was already happening to her, and she didn't want it to happen. To be able to think about Simon and not feel pain seemed like a betrayal, a denial of their love, and she never wanted to do that, ever.

'I don't want to hear any more of this,' she cried. 'I won't!'

'Kate, finding yourself attracted to another man—'

'I haven't—I haven't!' she said desperately. 'You have no right to say such things to me!'

'Kate—'

'I want to go, Dr Flett,' she said tightly, staring pointedly at his hand on her arm, 'and I want to go now.'

For a moment he said nothing, then he sighed and released her, but when she disappeared into the chalet he didn't follow her inside. Instead, he stayed outside, gazing down at the flower-filled meadow below.

He had never intended on kissing her but as soon as his lips had met hers all rational thought had disappeared from his mind. All he'd been aware of had been the gentle sweetness of her mouth, the high, soft swell of her breasts against his chest and his urgent, desperate need for her.

After Gemma had died he'd never even considered becoming involved with another woman. Oh, there'd been plenty who'd offered to 'comfort' him in his loneliness, but after eleven happy years of marriage the thought of sex without love, without some kind of commitment, hadn't appealed to him. In fact, no woman had appealed to him until he'd met a skinny, white-faced waif called Kate Rendall.

He wanted her, and it wasn't solely to make love to her. He wanted to take care of her. He wanted to erase the dark shadows that always lingered at the back of her eyes and, as he squared his jaw and turned to go into the chalet, he vowed that somehow, some way, he was going to make it happen.

CHAPTER FIVE

'You have three choices, Rhona. You can see one of the local doctors, you can let me examine you, or you can take a month's severance pay, starting from today.'

'Dr Flett—'

'Swallowing vast quantities of indigestion tablets isn't normal,' he interrupted, 'nor is persistent pain. If you want to continue working for me this pain has to be investigated—and investigated now.'

For a second the cook looked as though she might argue with him, then her shoulders slumped. 'All right,' she muttered. 'I'll see one of the local doctors.'

'I thought you might,' Ethan said, 'which is why I've made an appointment for you to see Dr Stollinger. He speaks excellent English so you'll have no trouble explaining your symptoms. The taxi will be here at ten, and your appointment's at half past.'

'This morning?' she gasped. 'But I need to get some groceries—'

'I'll get them for you,' Kate said quickly. 'If you give me a list of what you want, I'll go down to Kitzbühel and pick them up.'

Rhona glanced across at her for the first time since she'd come into the study, and her expression was cold.

'I'm surprised you need a list. You seem to have everything else so well organised—my life included.'

Kate flushed. It hadn't been easy, making up her mind to tell Ethan about her concern over Rhona's health, but when she'd noticed the woman bringing back yet another packet of indigestion tablets from Kitzbühel yesterday she'd known she couldn't delay any longer—even if

79

Ethan's method of dealing with the situation left a lot to be desired.

'Not exactly subtle, were you?' she said tightly when Rhona had gone. 'See a doctor or I'll sack you?'

'It worked, didn't it?' he remarked. 'Kate, if I hadn't given Rhona an ultimatum she would simply have agreed to see a doctor then conveniently ''forgotten'' about it.'

'Perhaps she would,' she retorted, 'but if that was an example of your bedside manner, all I can say is I hope you're never anywhere near mine.'

'Professionally or personally?'

His blue eyes were fixed on her and to her chagrin hot colour flooded into her cheeks.

'Both,' she managed to reply, before turning on her heel and making for the door.

'Kate.' All he'd said had been her name but somehow he'd managed to make it sound like both a caress and a tender rebuke, and she needed to take a long steadying breath before she could turn to face him.

'Kate, we have to talk about what happened in Kitzbühel.'

She didn't want to talk about what had happened in Kitzbühel and she took refuge in the only form of defence she had—attack.

'You might feel the need to, but personally I don't,' she replied, her voice clipped. 'I would prefer to try to forget the…the whole sordid episode.'

His dark eyebrows snapped down. 'My kissing you was sordid?'

Her colour deepened further. His kiss hadn't been sordid. It might have been devastating and shattering, but it hadn't been sordid. It was the dreams she'd been having since that were sordid. The dreams in which he made love to her so passionately that she woke bathed in sweat, her heart hammering in her chest.

'I have to go,' she said quickly. 'Rhona—'

'You didn't answer my question,' he broke in angrily. 'My kissing you was sordid?'

'Sordid—unforgivable—inexcusable,' she threw back at him, driven beyond endurance. 'You pick the correct adjective—I don't even want to think about it.'

And, without waiting for his reply, she swung out of the study and along the corridor, only to discover he had followed her.

'How many times do I have to tell you I don't want to discuss what happened?' she flared, rounding on him.

'Neither do I when you're behaving like this,' he replied, anger thickening his voice. 'It's about this shopping—'

'I told Rhona I'd deal with it, and I will.'

'How?'

'What do you mean—how?' she demanded, pushing open the veranda door to find Jodie still finishing her breakfast.

'Forgive me if I'm wrong,' he observed, 'but didn't you tell me the road terrified you?'

'Then it's about time I conquered that fear.'

'How very noble of you,' he said, his voice every bit as tight as hers, 'but even supposing you actually make it down to the town, just how—exactly—do you propose to buy this food?'

'From a shop, of course,' she retorted, all too conscious that Jodie was gazing from her to her father in wide-eyed astonishment. 'It's where people normally buy groceries.'

'And you're going to buy this food armed simply with a phrase book, are you?'

She hadn't thought of that. She hadn't thought of just how difficult it might be to explain what she wanted when she didn't speak the language.

'I'll manage,' she muttered.

His lip curled. 'I doubt that—I doubt it very much. I'll come with you and translate.'

'Dad, do we have to shop this morning?' Jodie asked,

pushing aside her empty cereal bowl and swallowing the last of her enzyme capsules. 'It's almost ten o'clock already, and I have a tennis lesson—'

'I'm sure missing one isn't going to blight your life,' her father retorted.

Jodie opened her mouth, then closed it again miserably, and Kate gritted her teeth. Just because he was angry with her didn't give him the right to take his temper out on his daughter.

And whose fault is it that he's angry? a little voice asked at the back of her mind.

Mine, she answered wretchedly. Mine because I said those dreadful things to him, and I only said them because I'm frightened.

She'd tried—God, how she'd tried over the last three days—to convince herself that he'd taken advantage of her, that he'd caught her at a vulnerable moment. But it wasn't true. He'd been right when he'd said she'd kissed him back. And she'd wanted to do a lot more than simply kiss him back.

Somehow—some way—he'd managed not only to breach the protective shell she'd built around herself when Simon had died but to drag her, kicking and screaming, into the present. And she didn't want to face the present. The past was safer.

There was one part of the present, however, that she couldn't ignore, and that was Jodie. No matter how she might feel, the girl shouldn't be made to suffer, and with a determined effort she smiled at her.

'It won't take me more than ten minutes to get a list of what we need from Rhona, and if we go down to Kitzbühel right away I'm sure we'll have all the shopping done well before eleven o'clock.'

Without even glancing in Ethan's direction, she strode quickly through the veranda door as fast as her trembling legs would take her.

*   *   *

It was a very strained journey down to Kitzbühel, and when they reached the shops it was even worse.

Ethan might have translated everything she wanted into German but he did it in such arctic tones that there were times when Kate was sorely tempted to go back to the car and leave him to it. Only the thought that he might accuse her of running away stopped her. That, and the sight of Jodie's deeply embarrassed and unhappy face as she trailed along behind them.

'Have we got everything?' Ethan asked when they finally began loading their purchases into the car.

Kate glanced down at her list. Jodie's diet was a high-energy one but she still had to ensure there was a balance between the sugary and fatty, energy-rich foods and the foods which provided protein and vitamins and minerals.

'I said, have we got everything?' Ethan repeated.

I'm not simple-minded, and I'm not deaf, Kate thought, staring steadfastly down at the list.

'I think so,' she said eventually, suddenly aware that Jodie was anxiously hopping from one foot to the other.

'Dad, it's a quarter to eleven. If I don't go now I'm going to be late for my lesson.'

'You won't.'

'I will. It'll take me fifteen minutes to walk to the tennis club and if I'm not there on time Franz will think I'm not coming and partner with someone else.'

'You won't be late because I'm driving you there,' her father said evenly. 'I want to meet this boy you keep talking about.'

Jodie's anguished expression, and Ethan's equally determined one, said it all and Kate's heart sank. She'd planned on having a quiet and solitary cup of coffee while Jodie was at the tennis courts, but Ethan had the look of a man who was about to launch into a heavy father act and there was no way she was going to let his daughter face that alone.

'I'll come with you,' she said quickly.

'There's no need,' Ethan replied, closing the boot with quite unnecessary force.

'I know there isn't,' she declared as evenly as she could, 'but I'd still like to come.'

'But—'

'I can walk to the tennis courts if you'd prefer,' she persevered, trying and failing to keep the edge out of her voice.

For a second she wondered if he was actually going to make her do just that, then without a word he got into the driver's seat and with singularly bad grace drove them all to the club.

The courts were busy with the usual mix of local and foreign youngsters but Kate had no difficulty in recognising Franz Zimmerman. Not only did he stand head and shoulders above the other teenagers, he also wore his long, blond hair tied back into a ponytail—a style which caused Ethan's eyebrows to lower ominously.

'So that's the famous Franz, is it?' he said as he watched Jodie join the boy on court. 'It's clearly high time he and I had a little chat.'

'I wouldn't,' Kate observed, making herself comfortable on one of the benches lining the court. 'Not if you want Jodie to continue speaking to you.'

'She can sulk all she likes,' he retorted. 'At fourteen she's far too young to be thinking about boyfriends.'

She shook her head at him in exasperation. 'Ethan, she's not a little girl any more. She'll be fifteen next week and it's perfectly natural for her to become interested in boys. If you wade in there, like some irate Victorian father—'

'So you're giving me lessons in parenthood now, are you?' he broke in, his blue eyes furious. 'It's not enough that you're determined to make me feel like some grubby pervert for kissing you, I'm also a lousy father as well! Well, that's rich coming from someone who's got no kids, nor is likely to have any, so I'd be grateful if in future you kept your damned thoughts and opinions to yourself!'

A heavy silence fell. A silence that was broken only by the twang of balls on rackets and the occasional exclamation of triumph or despair.

He was right, of course, Kate realised, gazing blindly at the white-clad figures in front of her. Jodie was his concern, not hers. She had no children and, as he'd so rightly pointed out, she was never likely to have any. Simon and she had always planned to have a family some time in the future but there had been no future, not for them.

With difficulty she swallowed the hard lump in her throat and heard him swear under his breath.

'Kate, I'm sorry. That crack—it was cheap and hurtful.'

'It's all right,' she murmured, staring steadfastly ahead, her throat constricted.

'It's not all right,' he said firmly.

Dimly she heard a faint rustling sound, then a piece of chocolate was suddenly thrust in front of her nose.

'Peace offering?'

Heaven only knew how long he'd had it, or what kind of chocolate it was. It had melted into a glutinous, unrecognisable mass but she took it from him without a word.

'I really am sorry, Kate,' he continued. 'Not for kissing you—you'll never make me feel sorry for that—but for what I said. It comes as a bit of a shock to be told that I don't always know what's best for my own child.'

She turned to him quickly. 'Ethan, you're a good father—a bit over-protective maybe—but your heart's in the right place. It's just that sometimes someone who's not so emotionally involved can see things you don't.'

He stared down at the chocolate, then up at her. 'Am I forgiven?'

She managed a lopsided smile. 'Give me another piece of that and I'll consider it.'

He chuckled, then his face grew serious. 'Kate, I really think we should talk.'

They did, she knew they did, but it was too soon, much too soon. How could she sit and calmly discuss something that had rocked her to her core—something she didn't fully understand even now?

Reluctantly she cleared her throat. 'Ethan—'

'*Guten Morgen, Katharina.*'

'Herr Zimmerman,' she said with ill-disguised relief, turning to see Franz's father striding towards them.

'How many times must I tell you my name is Gunther?' he chided, bending over her hand to kiss it. 'Herr Zimmerman is for my business colleagues and strangers— not for a lovely lady with eyes like brown velvet.'

His own eyes swept appreciatively over her and Kate could not stop herself from blushing. Gunther Zimmerman might be a practised flirt who exercised his not inconsiderable charm on all the female tourists who came to Kitzbühel, but a woman would have to have been made of stone not to be affected by the compliments of a blond-haired, six-foot-tall Adonis with an accent that made your toes curl.

'How are Jodie and Franz progressing with their lessons?' she asked, moving along the bench to make room for him.

'Steffi Graf and Boris Becker they are not, but they have fun, *ja*?' he replied, his eyes travelling past her and coming to rest on Ethan curiously.

Quickly Kate introduced the two men but it was obvious neither was impressed by what he saw. A brief handshake—and an even briefer nod—was their only acknowledgement and it was left to her to fill the silence when Gunther sat down.

'Jodie was telling me your son is going to London University this year?' she said.

He nodded. 'He is a clever boy. Not, I hasten to add,

that he inherited his brains from me. His mother—God rest her soul—was the intelligence in our family.'

'You are too modest, Gunther.' She smiled. 'You wouldn't own a chain of hotels in Kitzbühel if you were not a very intelligent man.'

He laughed. 'Tactful as well as beautiful—you are the perfect woman, Katharina.'

She chuckled and shook her head. She knew perfectly well she wasn't beautiful, but that didn't mean it wasn't nice to hear.

'I am glad we have met today,' he continued. 'I have a day off next Saturday and I wondered if you would like to visit Herrenchiemsee with me. It is one of Bavaria's most beautiful castles—'

'I'm taking Kate and Jodie to Herrenchiemsee next Saturday,' Ethan said quickly. 'It's my daughter's birthday.'

'Perhaps dinner that night, then?' Gunther ventured, gazing not at Ethan but at Kate.

'I'm afraid that's impossible, too,' Ethan declared before Kate could reply. 'We're all going out for dinner to the Schloss Berghof that evening.'

It was news to Kate that she was going to Herrenchiemsee and then out to dinner with Ethan and Jodie, but she managed to smile apologetically at Gunther.

'Perhaps some other time?' she said.

He nodded and got to his feet. 'That is a definite date. *Auf Wiedersehen*, Katharina. I will count the hours until we meet again.'

He was scarcely out of earshot before Ethan let out a very definite snort.

'"I will count the hours until we meet again,"' he mimicked in a mock-Austrian accent. 'What a load of old flannel!'

'I thought it was very pretty,' Kate said stiffly.

'Pretty?' he protested. 'Kate, that was one of the worst chat-up lines I've ever heard!'

She flushed. 'It wasn't a chat-up line. He was just being kind.'

'Kind be damned,' he retorted with irritation. 'It was a chat-up line.'

'And what if it was?' she could not help but flare. 'It's not a crime, is it?'

'No, but kissing you apparently is.'

'Ethan, please—'

'OK, OK,' he sighed in defeat as she gazed beseechingly at him.

'But we'll have to talk about it sometime, Kate.'

This year, next year, some time, never, she found herself thinking. And, please, please, make it never.

'And no going out on dates with Gunther in the meantime,' he continued, shooting her a warning glance. 'He's far too experienced for someone like you.'

She would have laughed if his comment hadn't been so ridiculous. Yes, Gunther had to be the most handsome man she'd ever met, paying her extravagant compliments which had her blushing furiously, but when he looked deep into her eyes she felt nothing, nothing at all, and yet with Ethan...

'What's so funny?' he demanded as she gave an involuntary chuckle.

'Life,' she replied with a slight smile. 'Just life.'

His eyebrows rose questioningly but there was no time to ask what she meant. Jodie had left the court and, though none of them would have admitted it, they were all anxious to get back to find out what Dr Stollinger had said to Rhona.

'He was very thorough—I'll say that for him,' the cook declared with a brightness that deceived nobody. 'Though why he felt the need to ask if I'd ever had whooping cough or rheumatic fever as a child is a mystery to me.'

'You must feel a lot happier, though, now you've seen him,' Ethan said.

'I felt perfectly happy before,' Rhona replied brusquely. 'I don't hold with being poked and prodded about—never have done.'

'It *is* for a good reason, Rhona,' he said gently. 'Once the results of your tests come back we'll know where we are.'

'If you say so,' she answered, looking anything but convinced. 'And now, if you'll excuse me, I have the washing-up to do.'

'No, you haven't,' he declared. 'You're taking the rest of the day off and relaxing.'

'But—'

'Doctor's orders, Rhona—*this* doctor's orders.'

Kate waited until the cook had safely left the sitting-room, before shaking her head. 'Blood tests, auscultation, chest X-rays and an ECG. He thinks she's got heart disease, doesn't he?'

'I know Rhona had rheumatic fever as a child.' Ethan frowned. 'And I'm guessing he suspects she might have mitral incompetence—thickening and scarring of the mitral valve.'

'But if the mitral valve isn't closing properly, and blood is leaking back into the left atrium—the upper chamber of the heart—shouldn't she be very breathless?' Kate queried.

'Not necessarily,' he replied. 'It's amazing how the heart can compensate for a defect like that, and the damage caused by rheumatic fever can sometimes take years to appear.'

'But, Ethan, if the blood keeps on flowing back into the left atrium—'

'The build-up of blood could lead to left-sided heart failure and pulmonary oedema,' he finished for her.

She got to her feet and went over to the window. 'What are we going to do?'

'Nothing until we get the results of the tests back.'

'And then, if it is mitral incompetence?'

He came and stood beside her, his expression pensive. 'If she were my patient, and the damage wasn't severe, I'd prescribe diuretics to reduce the fluid in the lungs, one of the digitalis drugs to increase the force of the heart's contractions and anti-coagulants to prevent blood clots. Many people live quite happily for years with the condition, but even if she requires surgery the success rate for the operation is excellent.'

'That isn't what I meant,' she said. 'Ethan, I think we should all go home—back to Malden.'

'I think Rhona should certainly go home. Think about it, Kate,' he continued as she opened her mouth to protest. 'If it is mitral incompetence and we all go back to Malden she'll only work herself up into a state, thinking she's spoilt our holiday.'

He was right, but the thought of staying on in the chalet with just Ethan and Jodie for company filled her with dread.

'But who'll cook for us if Rhona goes home?' she asked, desperately clutching at straws. 'Much as I'd like to help—'

'I'll do it.'

'You can cook?'

The amazed words were out of her mouth before she could stop them and she coloured faintly as he chuckled.

'Of course I can cook—and very well, as it happens. Did you think I wouldn't know one end of a can-opener from the other?'

'I hadn't thought about it at all,' she confessed. 'I just assumed—the Harley Street practice, this chalet…'

'You assumed I was some pampered millionaire who wouldn't know how to boil an egg if his life depended on it?' he suggested. 'Kate, my mother and father were impoverished school teachers, and I had to work my way through university living mostly on beans and toast. The Harley Street practice wasn't mine. An old friend from med school heard I was looking for a position and offered me a job, working for him.'

'And the chalet?' she asked.

'A gift from a very rich, very spoilt patient after I'd told her she didn't have heart disease but should lay off the olives with her gin.'

'I don't believe you.' She laughed.

'It's as true as I'm sitting here,' he protested.

'What is?' Jodie asked curiously as she came into the sitting-room.

'That your father is an incredibly talented, handsome, modest man.' He grinned.

'Oh, yeah, right,' she said, rolling her eyes. 'How did Rhona get on at the doctor's?'

'Fine. She's a bit anxious about the tests she's had, but I've told her there's no need to worry.'

Jodie screwed up her nose. 'Doctors! Nothing but qualified vampires, the lot of them—always wanting to take blood for this and blood for that.'

He chuckled. 'So, what's our itinerary for this afternoon, then?'

'I don't care what we do as long as we don't go anywhere near a church or a museum,' his daughter said firmly.

'No churches or museums it is,' her father said, winking across at Kate. 'What about a few rounds of crazy golf at the course in town? You used to love playing that.'

Jodie gazed at him witheringly. 'That was when I was a kid, Dad.'

'Oh, poor old lady!' He grinned.

'Why don't we go up the Kitzbüheler Horn on the cable car?' she suggested. 'There's a restaurant and a gift shop at the top, and on a clear day you can see all the way to Lake Chiemsee in Bavaria.'

'Would you like that, Kate?' Ethan asked, smiling across at her.

She would. In fact, she suddenly realised with dismay that she really didn't mind what they did as long as the three of them did it together.

When had it happened? When had she started to feel like part of this family instead of simply the hired nurse? And she did feel like a member of the family. She cared a great deal for Jodie, and as for Ethan…

She didn't want to analyse what her feelings were for him. Analysing them meant admitting she had them, and *that* she didn't want to face right now.

'Look, why don't you make this afternoon just a father-and-daughter outing?' she said quickly.

'But, Kate—'

'I think perhaps we've imposed on Kate's good nature too much already, Jodie,' her father interrupted abruptly, the smile on his face fading. 'She probably has other things she'd like to do.'

'You don't, do you, Kate?' Jodie asked. 'Come with us, *please*—it won't be the same without you.'

'Stop it, Jodie,' her father ordered. 'Kate is entitled to some time on her own.'

And she was, she told herself. She wasn't paid to be with Jodie twenty-four hours a day, seven days a week. Then tell him you have other things to do, a little voice whispered at the back of her mind, but as she deliberately shifted her gaze away from him and her eyes fell on Jodie's anxious, too-thin face, she heard herself say, 'OK. I'll come.'

'It's breathtaking!' Kate exclaimed as she hung over the observation platform, her eyes glowing. 'I can't believe that lake we can see is in Bavaria. And the Alps, Ethan—look at the Alps. They're even more stunning close up than they are in the valley. And smell that pine forest—it's so sharp, so clean, so…so…'

'Breathtaking?' he suggested, his lips curving with amusement.

'Sorry,' she said, her cheeks flushing slightly. 'You must think I'm a proper idiot.'

'Kate, I think you're wonderful,' he said softly.

He meant it. She could see it in the warmth of his eyes, the tender smile on his lips, and she looked away quickly, completely unable to meet his gaze.

'Dad, I could really murder an ice cream,' Jodie exclaimed, jumping up on the observation platform to join them.

'You're hungry again?' he protested. 'OK, OK,' he went on with a grin as she scowled at him. 'Kate, would you like a coffee?'

'Only if I can have it out here,' she replied. 'This view is so stunning I don't want to miss it for a second.'

'Out here it will be,' he declared, leading the way over to one of the tables.

'I didn't realise Herrenchiemsee castle—the castle Gunther was talking about—is actually situated in the middle of that lake we can see,' Kate observed as they sat down.

Ethan nodded. 'It was built by King Ludwig II of Bavaria in 1878...'

He came to a halt and let out a low, muttered oath.

'What is it?' Kate asked, twisting round in her seat to see what had caused his annoyance.

'Does that wretched boy haunt us?' he said in exasperation as Franz Zimmerman came out of the restaurant. 'OK, OK,' he added as Jodie leapt to her feet and rushed over to him and Kate shook her head, 'if she brings him over I'll keep my mouth shut.'

'You'd better,' she warned. 'I don't know how high up we are here but I'd hate for you to reach the town the fast way.'

He chuckled but his eyebrows rose in surprise when

Jodie rejoined them alone. 'Isn't he coming over to say hello?'

'He's got someone with him.'

Something about Jodie's voice caused Kate to look over her shoulder again. The someone Franz had with him was a buxom girl of about seventeen with a cascade of auburn curls.

'She's probably his sister,' she said, recognising the signs of deep adolescent anguish on Jodie's face.

'She's not. Her name's Marta Schieber, and her father owns a construction company in Kitzbühel.'

'Pretty girl,' Ethan observed, staring over at the couple.

'Yes,' Jodie muttered flatly.

'Personally I think you're a lot prettier,' Kate declared, aiming a kick under the table at Ethan's shins and hitting the table leg instead.

'Gorgeous hair,' Ethan continued. 'Nice eyes, too.'

Kate attempted another kick and this time, judging by Ethan's startled pained expression, made contact.

'Personally,' she said determinedly, '*personally*, I think she's a little bit obvious. That sweater she's wearing for a start... Ethan, you're a man. Don't you think her sweater's a little bit obvious?'

He gazed at her in confusion for a moment, then began to nod vigorously. 'Oh, absolutely. Far too revealing— much too revealing.'

'At least she's got something to reveal,' Jodie said bitterly. 'I'm fifteen next week and I still haven't got any boobs and my periods haven't started yet. When am I going to start developing properly, Dad?'

For some reason Ethan's blue shirt suddenly seemed rather tight around his neck and his chair didn't appear all that comfortable either.

'What on earth's happened to our coffees?' he said, gazing in the direction of the restaurant as a sailor might regard a lighthouse on a stormy night. 'The time that man's taking with them he could have ground the beans by hand.'

'Dad, you didn't answer my question,' Jodie persisted. 'When are my boobs—'

'Not now, sweetheart,' he interrupted, getting quickly to his feet. 'Right now I want to find out what's happened to our drinks.'

Jodie watched him go, a wry expression on her face. 'Exit stage left, one deeply embarrassed father.'

Kate chuckled. 'Don't be too hard on him. He's just finding it a bit difficult to accept you're growing up.'

'But I'm not—that's the whole point,' Jodie protested. 'I'm as flat-chested as I was two years ago. When is my figure going to start developing, like other girls'?'

Kate sighed. 'Girls who have CF always develop a lot more slowly, but I promise you'll begin developing breasts soon and your periods will start, too.'

Jodie took one of the paper napkins out of the glass container on the table and began pleating it into a fan. 'Dr Torrance…he gave me this leaflet about puberty and sex and stuff, and it said…,it said boys with CF were usually sterile.'

'You're a girl, not a boy,' Kate said firmly. 'Once your periods start you could get pregnant just as easily as any other girl—though I wouldn't advise you consider doing that for a quite a few years yet,' she added as interest gleamed in Jodie's eyes.

'Would my baby have CF?'

'It would depend upon whether you and the father were carriers of the gene or not. Having CF yourself doesn't necessarily mean you're a carrier.'

'You explain it a whole heap better than Dr Torrance ever did,' Jodie commented, then pushed her seat back. 'Look, do you mind if I take a quick look in the gift shop and see if they might have anything that would suit Aunt Di? Dad hates shopping, you see…'

'Go on—I'll be fine,' Kate said with a smile.

With an answering grin Jodie began to walk away, only to pause and come back. 'Kate, I just want to say… The thing is, I know I was a real pain when you first came to Malden, but, well, since I've got to know you I just want to say I think you're OK.'

'Why, thank you, Jodie,' she replied, quite taken aback. 'I think you're pretty OK, too.'

And she did, she realised, her throat tight as she watched the girl make her way towards the gift shop. Jodie might drive her mad at times with her moods and tempers, but she couldn't have been more fond of her if she'd been her own daughter.

'Is that the facts-of-life chat done?'

She looked up to see Ethan holding out a cup of coffee to her, his eyes dancing, and managed to smile.

'You're out of luck, I'm afraid,' she replied. 'Breasts, periods and having a baby were the topics for today. How you actually conceived the baby wasn't on the agenda.'

He stared down at her for a moment, then his eyes narrowed. 'OK, what happened? Was Jodie rude to you?'

'No—oh, no.' She smiled again, this time a little tremulously. 'I was just thinking how very lucky you are. Simon and I—we always planned to have a family, but…'

He sat down opposite her, his blue eyes fixed on hers. 'It's still not too late, Kate.'

No, it wasn't, she thought as somewhere deep inside her she felt the tight band which had been round her heart since Simon died loosen slightly. It wasn't too late because, try as she might, she couldn't keep on pretending that what she felt for the man sitting opposite her was all in her imagination or the delusions of an exhausted brain.

Her feelings were real, and they weren't going to go away. The only trouble was that she didn't know whether she had the courage to do anything about them.

CHAPTER SIX

'ACCORDING to this guide book, King Ludwig used to spend huge amounts of money putting on productions of plays and then watching them all by himself. Is that weird, or what?'

'Maybe he suffered from claustrophobia, sweetheart,' Ethan said, pulling out to overtake a slow-moving tractor.

'He was weird,' Jodie said firmly, closing the guide book with a snap. She gazed out of the car window for a moment, then sighed. 'Is it much further to Herrenchiemsee?'

'The landing stage is just up there.'

'Thank God for that. I feel like I've been stuck in this car for hours—how about you, Kate?'

'I'm fine,' she answered.

'You're sure?' Jodie pressed, turning round in the front passenger seat to look at her. 'You've been awfully quiet all morning.'

'I've been admiring the countryside,' she replied quickly.

And wishing I could have come up with a really good excuse to get out of this trip, she added mentally.

Nothing she'd tried had worked. She'd tried pleading tiredness and Jodie had simply said the day out would do her good. She'd tried suggesting she'd seen more than enough historic monuments since she'd come to Austria, and Jodie had merely observed that Herrenchiemsee wasn't any old monument but one of the wonders of Bavaria. And she didn't want to let Jodie down on her birthday.

And Ethan had been no help at all, she recalled. He'd simply stood in silence, listening to her increasingly feeble excuses with a maddening smile playing around on his lips.

The maddening smile was still there when they reached

the landing stage and Jodie dashed off to get their tickets for the short boat trip across to the island.

'You can relax, Kate,' he said. 'I'm not going to jump on you.'

'I—I never thought for one minute that you were,' she stuttered.

'No?' he said dryly. 'Kate, I kissed you once and you told me you didn't enjoy the experience. I have no intention of kissing you again until you tell me that you want me to.'

She noticed he hadn't said he wouldn't ever kiss her again and warm colour spread across her cheeks. 'Ethan—'

'Kate, if I'd intended having my wicked way with you I certainly wouldn't have planned a long and tiring car drive first, nor would I have brought my daughter along as a spectator.'

A wobbly chuckle sprang from her lips and he nodded approvingly.

'That's better. Now, for heaven's sake, relax and enjoy the day.'

She'd have found it an awful lot easier if Gunther had been with her, she thought ruefully. Gunther wore shorts all the time and yet her eyes didn't keep straying to his legs the way her eyes seemed irresistibly drawn to Ethan's hard, muscled thighs. And Gunther's smile didn't make her feel tense and vulnerable, and completely ill-equipped to handle the feelings she was experiencing.

Relax, she told herself as they took the short boat trip across to the island and she stood as far away from Ethan as she could. Relax, she repeated when his arm accidentally brushed against hers while they were walking through the small wood that led to the castle. But the minute she saw Herrenchiemsee all her reservations about coming on this trip disappeared and all she could think was how very glad she was to have come.

'Impressed?' Ethan grinned, hearing her gasp out loud.

'It's incredible,' she said truthfully.

'King Ludwig was a great admirer of King Louis XIV of France—the monarch they called the Sun King because of the magnificence of his court,' he explained as he led the way up the wide stone steps, 'so he modelled Herrenchiemsee on King Louis's palace at Versailles.'

Kate didn't know whether the castle was modelled on Versailles or not. All she knew, as Ethan guided them through room after room full of ornate furniture and priceless Meissen china, was that Herrenchiemsee was the most beautiful place she'd ever seen.

'It must have cost an absolute fortune to build,' she observed when they stopped to admire a particularly fine piece of sculpture.

'It did.' Ethan nodded. 'King Ludwig is known either as the ''Fairy Tale King'' or the ''Mad King'' depending on your point of view. He point-blank refused to spend any money on armaments and spent all of Bavaria's income on art and music.'

'Sounds like a sensible man to me,' Jodie declared, squinting down to admire the fine detail on the statue.

'A lot of people at his court didn't think so—especially when he kept on building hugely expensive castles and supporting composers like Wagner. The final straw came when he began to spend more and more of his time working on inventions like that dining-room table we saw, which could be winched up fully laden with food from the kitchen so that he didn't have to see anyone.'

'What happened to him?' Kate asked.

'I know the answer to that,' Jodie declared before her father could reply. 'He was declared insane and unfit to rule when he was forty-one and two days after his birthday he and the doctor who was supposed to be looking after him were found drowned in Lake Starnberg. Now, is that suspicious, or what?'

'I think it's sad,' Kate replied. 'The poor man—after creating so much beauty—to die like that.'

'Yeah, right,' Jodie agreed, 'but can we get something to eat soon because I'm starving?'

'Oh, Jodie, where's the romance in your soul, the poetry in your heart?' Ethan laughed, cuffing his daughter gently under the chin.

'Can't hear it for the rumbling in my tummy.' She grinned, and her father shook his head and laughed again.

'I thought we might just buy some rolls and fruit to eat out in the gardens as we're going out to dinner tonight, if that's all right with you, Kate?' he said as he led the way down the stairs and out of the castle.

'Suits me fine,' she answered. 'I've got Jodie's enzyme capsules with me and some extra crisps…' She stopped, suddenly aware that Jodie wasn't with them any more, and turned to see her with her nose pressed up against the gift shop window.

'Typical woman,' Ethan groaned as they walked back to her. 'Show her culture and she complains about being hungry. Show her a shop and she's in there like a ferret.'

'Oh, ha, ha, very funny,' Kate said. 'Have you seen something interesting, Jodie?'

'You bet,' she replied. 'That book in the window—the history of Bavarian costume. Dad, I really, really like it, but I'm a bit overspent on my weekly allowance—'

'Four weeks overspent, to be exact, young lady,' he interrupted. 'Jodie, I bought you all those clothes for your birthday, and I'm taking you to the Schloss Berghof this evening for dinner—'

'And I really appreciate it, Dad,' she said, her large blue eyes fixed guilelessly on him, 'and the clothes are great— the best ever—but if you could maybe see your way to buying me this book I'll never ask for anything ever again.'

Kate chuckled inwardly. There wasn't a daughter born who couldn't wrap her father round her little finger when she wanted to, and Jodie was no exception. Ethan might grumble and complain, but she knew the minute he agreed to take a look at the book it was as good as bought.

'Ethan—those lockets in the window,' she said when he and Jodie eventually came out of the shop, with Jodie triumphantly clutching her book. 'The ones with the edelweiss engraved on them—how many schillings did you say there were to the pound?'

He told her and she stood for some moments, clearly working out elaborate calculations in her head, then sighed. 'OK, let's go.'

'Don't you want to go in—take a proper look at them?' he asked.

She shook her head. 'They're way out of my price range. Come on, we'd better eat before Jodie starts complaining in earnest.'

He nodded absently, then seemed to come to a decision. 'Look, there's a quiet spot by the edge of those trees near the formal gardens. Why don't you and Jodie make yourselves comfortable, and I'll pick up the rolls?'

'But—'

'There's no sense in us all standing in line,' he interrupted. 'I'll see you in about ten minutes, OK?'

It would take considerably longer than that, she thought, watching him go. Not only would he have to wait to be served, he'd have to somehow carry all the food and drink for them on his own, but if that was what he wanted she could hardly argue.

'That dress and all the other clothes you got my dad to buy me are really terrific,' Jodie commented when they reached the spot Ethan had indicated and sat down on the grass. 'I can't wait to get dressed up tonight.'

'This place we're going to—the Schloss Berghof—is it nice?' Kate asked.

'And how. Rhona's really missing out by having dinner with that couple she's got so friendly with, but I don't suppose she minds—she gets uncomfortable in posh places.'

'Posh?' Kate repeated. 'This place is posh?'

'You bet. I remember the manager once refusing to let somebody in because he wasn't wearing a dinner suit.'

Kate mentally flicked through the contents of her wardrobe and panicked. What in the world was she going to wear? The only clothes she'd brought with her to Austria apart from casual clothes were summer dresses.

The red one, she decided. It had a heart-shaped neckline, sleeves that ended just below her elbows and a skirt that brushed her calves. By no stretch of the imagination could it ever have been described as evening wear but it was either wear that or pretend to have a headache, and she had a horrible suspicion if she tried the latter Jodie would simply stuff aspirin down her throat and insist she still come.

Determinedly she pushed all thoughts of that evening out of her mind as Ethan approached, laden with packages. Relax and enjoy the day, Ethan had told her, and she had enjoyed it, as she confessed after they'd eaten their lunch and Jodie had wandered off to take some photographs of the gardens before they went home.

'It's so very beautiful here,' she observed, leaning back contentedly against one of the trees, 'and that was a lovely lunch, even if you did buy enough to feed an army.'

'Di instructed me to fatten you up, remember?' he said, then shook his head as his eyes travelled over her. 'I don't seem to be having much success, do I?'

'I've always been skinny,' she replied, wrapping her arms round her bare knees and suddenly wishing she'd worn a skirt—a very long skirt—instead of the shorts she'd put on.

'Slender,' he said, getting to his feet and coming to sit beside her. 'I'd call you petite and slender.'

'My brother called me scrawny Kate when we were

kids,' she said with a shaky laugh, wishing he'd stayed where he was.

'Your brother was clearly a philistine.'

'And if it wasn't scrawny Kate, it was scrubby Kate because I always looked as though I'd been dragged through a hedge backwards,' she continued, trying desperately not to notice that one of his bare, brown, muscular thighs was lying scarcely an inch away from her own. 'Mind you, I got my own back. I called him drippy Drew.'

'Sounds like he deserved it,' he murmured, his breath a faint whisper against her cheek.

'H-he wasn't that bad really,' she managed to reply, steadfastly keeping her gaze fixed on the castle in front of them. 'H-he could be a bit pompous at times—still is, in fact.'

'I'd like to meet this brother of yours.'

'M-maybe you will one day,' she floundered, feeling her stomach tighten as he stretched out to brush a stray piece of grass from her leg.

'Maybe I will at that,' he said, his voice a low caress.

She could feel her heart hammering hard against her chest and a shiver of expectation ran down her spine. He was going to kiss her, she was sure he was, but when he didn't move, didn't do anything, she was forced to turn her head to look at him.

'This time you ask, Kate,' he said softly, his blue eyes fixed on hers. 'That's what I said, didn't I—that I would only kiss you again if you asked me to?'

She nodded, unable to say a word, scarcely able even to breathe.

'I'm a patient man, Kate,' he continued, 'but even patient men have their limits. By the end of today I want you either to tell me that if I don't keep my grubby little hands to myself you'll leave my employment, or…'

'Or?' she whispered.

'You admit you want me as much as I want you and we

decide what we're going to do about it. And now,' he added, as they both saw Jodie waving from in front of the castle, 'we'd better start making tracks. Our table at the Schloss Berghof is booked for seven and I expect you want time to get your glad rags on.'

What I want, she thought, getting shakily to her feet, is time to decide what I'm going to do. And time—as Ethan had just made all too abundantly clear—was the one thing he wasn't offering.

The Schloss Berghof was every bit as exclusive as Jodie had said. Chandeliers glittered and gleamed from the ceilings, there wasn't a piece of furniture that wasn't antique, and the dining room was full of men in immaculate dinner suits and women in beautiful evening gowns.

That their entrance caused no little comment was clear. Several of the diners nudged one another as they made their way towards their table. Automatically Kate stiffened her shoulders and tried to look as though she dined in places like this every night of the week.

They're probably not looking at you anyway, she told herself. They're probably wondering who the good-looking man and pretty young girl are, but as the evening progressed she realised it wasn't Jodie and Ethan that kept so many eyes riveted to their table. It was her.

It's because I'm wrongly dressed, she told herself as she tried to enjoy the Gerüchertes Forellenfilet Ethan had chosen for her which, despite its fearsome name, turned out to be a delicious smoked fillet of trout served with whipped cream and horseradish. It's because they know my dress could be bought in any high-street chain store, she thought as she looked up from her chocolate meringue to find the eyes of several of the female diners still on her.

But when the coffee and cheese arrived and the intense scrutiny still hadn't ended she knew there must be something else. She had just turned to Ethan to ask him about it when to her surprise Gunther appeared at their table.

'Happy birthday, Fraülein Jodie.' He beamed, bowing gallantly over her hand and kissing it.

'Is Franz with you, Herr Zimmerman?' she asked eagerly, peering round his tall form to scan the tables.

'He is indeed, my dear, which is why I am here,' he declared. 'I have been sent as an emissary to crave a boon of your father.'

'Indeed?' Ethan said dryly.

'Franz and some of his friends are going on to a disco and we wondered if Jodie would like to join them as it's her birthday. She would be quite safe, I assure you,' Gunther continued as a frown appeared on Ethan's forehead. 'I and some of the other parents are going along as chaperons.'

'Can I go—oh, please, Dad?' Jodie breathed, her eyes shining. 'I'd really like to.'

For a moment Ethan said nothing, then he nodded. 'OK, but I want you back at the chalet by eleven o'clock.'

'Dad, it's already nine o'clock,' she protested. 'The disco will hardly have got started yet. Make it one o'clock.'

'Half past eleven.'

'Midnight?' she suggested hopefully, and he laughed.

'Midnight it is—but not a minute later, understand?'

It was doubtful whether Jodie even heard him. She was already rushing out of the dining room and Ethan shook his head.

'I suppose this is just a sample of what I've got to look forward to when we go back to Malden—discos, rave-ups, parties.'

Kate chuckled, then glanced at him curiously. 'Have you lost something?' she asked, seeing him searching through the pockets of his dinner jacket.

'Not lost something—looking for. Ah, here it is.'

'What's this?' she asked in surprise as he put a small box down by her plate.

'Open it and see. It's a present, Kate,' he continued as she gazed at him in confusion. 'Go on, open it.'

Quickly she did as he requested and gasped when her eyes fell on one of the lockets she'd admired that morning. 'Ethan, I can't accept this. It's far too expensive.'

'It's a gift, Kate, and you can either look on it as a going-away gift or a welcome-to-a-new-life gift. The choice is yours.'

'A going-away gift?' she said faintly.

'I said I wanted your decision before the end of the day, and if you've decided that all we can ever be to one another is employer and employee it's best if we part company right now because I can't go on like this, feeling the way I do about you.'

'Ethan—'

'I mean it, Kate,' he said, his face implacable. 'The choice is yours.'

'Do I have to make it here—now?' she said, trying to buy time, and he sighed.

'We'll go back to the chalet if it's privacy you want, but make no mistake, my dear, one way or another you're going to have to make up your mind tonight.'

Reluctantly she got to her feet and followed him out to the car. She was attracted to him—she couldn't deny it. When he touched her she seemed to melt, when he'd kissed her that day she'd wanted him with a ferocity which had shocked her, but to go that one step further—to take that one very big step further... She honestly didn't know whether she could, and yet the alternative—to leave his employment, never see him again—chilled her very soul.

Neither of them spoke as Ethan carefully negotiated the twisting, winding road that led back to the chalet. Both sat lost in their own thoughts, and it was only when he slammed on his brakes and she had to put out her hands to stop herself from hitting the dashboard that she saw what he must have seen a few seconds earlier—a car, lying on its side in a gully beside the road.

'Stay where you are,' he called, leaping out of the car. 'It might catch fire so let me check it out first.'

Like heck I will, she thought, scrambling out and following him towards the crumpled wreckage of the vehicle.

Miraculously the driver—a young man in his late twenties—was still alive and quickly Kate checked his airways.

'No blood in his mouth,' she murmured as she leaned carefully over him. 'Breathing shallow but not worryingly so.'

'I'm a British doctor and my companion's a qualified nurse,' Ethan said as the young man suddenly groaned. 'Can you tell us your name?'

'Ian—Ian Berkeley.'

'You're British?'

'Yes, I'm British. Look—'

'Do you know where you are?'

'What?'

'I said do you know where you are?' Ethan repeated.

'Of course I know where I am,' the young man exclaimed. 'I'm in Austria, on the first day of my annual holiday, stuck in my damn car after a crash, OK?'

Ethan grinned across at Kate and she smiled back. Ethan's questions might have sounded ridiculous but the more answers Ian Berkeley could give to his questions, the greater was his level of consciousness.

'I think he's broken his leg,' Kate murmured as Ethan pocketed his mobile phone, having dialled 144 to call for an ambulance. 'But apart from that and some facial lacerations, I'd say he's got off pretty lightly.'

'Pulse?'

Quickly Kate took it, then frowned.

'Something wrong?' Ethan asked.

'It must be my watch,' she muttered. 'I'll take it again.'

'Look, pardon me for butting in,' the young man said, 'but do you think you could maybe do something useful, like getting me out of here instead of fiddling and faddling about with my pulse?'

'We would if we could,' Ethan declared soothingly, 'but we don't have a cervical collar, and I'd rather not move you unless it was an emergency. We could damage your spine, you see.'

Ian Berkeley subsided into silence and Kate stepped back from the car, motioning to Ethan to follow her.

'OK, what's wrong?' he asked, seeing her furrowed brow.

'His pulse,' she replied, lowering her voice. 'Ethan, it's ninety.'

'It can't be,' he protested. 'That's way too high for the injuries he's sustained.'

'I know.' She nodded. 'That's why I took it twice—I was sure I must have made a mistake, but I haven't.'

'Internal injuries,' he muttered. 'He must have internal injuries that we can't see and his body's producing its own endorphins so he doesn't feel any pain.'

Quickly he went back to the car.

'Would you mind if I took another look at you, Ian?' he asked.

'Feel free,' the young man replied. 'It appears I'm not going anywhere at the moment.'

'So, what line of work are you in, Ian?' Kate asked, deliberately making conversation as Ethan lightly ran his hands over him.

'I'm a teacher. I've been saving up all year for this holiday and I only arrived in Austria this morning—haven't even checked into my hotel yet.'

'Is there anyone you'd like us to phone—your family back home, for example—to tell them what's happened?' Kate asked, noticing Ethan's eyes narrow when his fingers reached the young man's stomach.

'Haven't got any family,' Ian replied. 'I suppose you'd better phone my school—tell them I'm not going to be back at work next week.' His eyes suddenly gleamed. 'Hey, you know they're right about every cloud having a silver lining. This accident means old Jenkins will have to get off his fat butt and take my classes. Thank you, God.'

And thank you, God, for sending the ambulance so quickly, Kate thought, sighing inwardly with relief as she heard the familiar wail of the high-pitched siren.

Her relief, however, was short-lived. After rapidly explaining the situation in German to the doctor and accompanying paramedics, Ethan suddenly let fly with a string of expletives which she didn't have to be able to speak German to understand.

'What is it—what's wrong?' she asked as the paramedics carefully lifted Ian Berkeley out of the car and onto a stretcher.

'They're taking him to St Joseph's in Salzburg,' he said furiously. 'Kate, he has an abdominal aneurysm. I felt it when I was examining him and it's big enough to rupture at any minute.'

'You mean…?'

He nodded. 'If he hadn't had this accident he could have collapsed and died at any minute, and now those idiots are taking him to Salzburg because there's no qualified surgeon on call at the weekends in Kitzbühel.'

'But if it's set to rupture—'

'He won't make the journey,' he finished for her grimly, before turning quickly back to the young doctor.

Another rapid conversation took place, which seemed to involve a lot of head-shaking and considerably more highly colourful remarks from Ethan, judging by the open-mouthed expressions of the paramedics.

'What's happening now?' Kate demanded as the young doctor shrugged in apparent defeat and got into the ambulance.

'They're taking him to Kitzbühel.'

'But you said there was no qualified surgeon there,' she protested, almost having to run to keep up with him as he strode towards their car. 'Have they sent for a specialist?'

'He's already here—it's me.'

She came to a dead halt in the centre of the road. *'You?'*

'Kate, it was the only way I could persuade them,' he said, his eyes begging for her understanding. 'If he goes to Salzburg he'll die before he gets there. This way I can give him a chance.'

Yes, he could give him a chance, she thought, staring up at him, and if the operation was a success it would be congratulations all round, but if Ian died... If he died they'd crucify the foreign doctor who had operated on him in a country that wasn't his own.

She took a deep breath. 'Any room in the operating theatre for a slightly rusty theatre sister?'

He gazed, open-mouthed, at her for a second, then vigorously shook his head. 'No—no way. Kate, if I don't pull this off, I'm not taking you down with me.'

'Rubbish,' she said stoutly. 'I know you—you just want to hog all the limelight yourself.'

'Kate—'

'The ambulance left three minutes ago,' she pointed out, 'so are you going to operate or spend the rest of the night standing here, arguing with me?'

He stared at her impotently then a glimmer of a smile appeared in his eyes. 'You're insane. You know that, don't you?'

'Then that makes two of us,' she said with a smile. 'Now, come on—we've got a patient waiting.'

The journey didn't take long. The blaring siren and the ability of both the ambulance driver and Ethan to travel the tortuous road at breakneck speed saw to that. Once at the hospital the X-ray department swiftly confirmed Ethan's diagnosis and, with a blood match taken and the anaesthetist and theatre staff standing by, Kate and Ethan needed simply to scrub up and the operation could proceed.

It was then that the enormity of what they were doing hit Kate. She had no doubts whatsoever as to Ethan's skill, but it had been four years since he'd operated on anyone and three years since she'd been in an operating theatre. Please, she prayed. Please, let it be all right. Please, let us both remember what we're supposed to do and must do.

Within seconds of her handing him the first instrument, and him making his first incision, she knew her fears had been groundless. The years simply fell away and it was as though neither of them had ever been anywhere else but in an operating theatre.

'It's a big one,' Ethan murmured as he dissected around the aorta above the aneurysm and then passed the long right-angle clamp Kate handed to him gently behind it.

It was. A normal aorta should have been between two and three centimetres in diameter. This one was at least four and a half centimetres. It could rupture at any minute but at least now, after Ethan had pulled a long, wet piece of tape round it and clipped the two ends together with a haemostat, it would be possible to stop any haemorrhage by tightening the tape.

'Crafoord clamp,' Ethan muttered after he had cleared the tissue around the aneurysm.

Quickly she handed it to him, knowing that once the clamp was closed around the aorta above the aneurysm Ethan would have to work very fast indeed because no arterial blood would be passing to the lower part of Ian Berkeley's body.

'He was certainly living on borrowed time,' Ethan observed as Kate placed another clamp below the aneurysm so he could slit down through the middle of the aneurysm.

Borrowed time was right, Kate thought. The walls of the aorta were paper thin, with only a narrow channel remaining open—and that was full of blood clot. Ian's only hope was that the tubular graft made of plastic which Ethan was going to insert to replace the dilated aneurysm would hold.

'Check for backflow?' she asked as he paused with a few stitches still remaining to be inserted.

He nodded and gently she released the lower clamp for a second. To her relief there didn't seem to be any air in the graft and the blood was welling up nicely.

'Looks good so far,' he said.

She nodded silently and after he'd inserted the last stitches she carefully removed the bottom clamp.

'Moment-of-truth time, eh?' He grinned behind his mask as he reached for the top clamp.

She held her breath as he released it slowly, watching for leaks, and hers wasn't the only sigh of relief that rippled round the operating theatre when it held.

There was one thing left to do. Quickly she moved down to the bottom of the operating table to check the pulses in Ian's ankles to see if the blood was circulating as it should. If his legs became a dark mottled blue it meant that the graft had clotted, and if it had clotted there was nothing they could do. To operate again would almost certainly kill him.

'Well?' Ethan asked, his face for the first time showing signs of fatigue.

'Very well.' She beamed. 'Congratulations, Doctor.'

He talked about the operation all the way back to the chalet. He was still talking about it when they finally got out of the car and made their way to the sitting-room.

'You enjoyed that, didn't you?' she asked when he finally drew breath. 'I don't mean you were pleased Ian had his accident and then discovering the aneurysm—but you enjoyed operating, didn't you?'

He gazed down at her silently for a moment, then his eyes lit up. 'I'd forgotten what it was like, Kate. The adrenaline rush, the buzz, the sheer *excitement* of operating on someone and knowing you'd saved their life.'

'You should go back to work,' she said softly. 'I don't mean full time—I'd never suggest that,' she added quickly as his face set. 'But perhaps part-time, in somewhere like Newcastle so you'd be close to home if you were needed.'

'Perhaps,' he murmured.

'You're a good surgeon, Ethan,' she continued, 'and, much as I hate to say it, your sister was right. Jodie doesn't need you twenty-four hours a day but people like Ian Berkeley desperately need your skill.'

'Perhaps,' he said again.

'Rhona doesn't seem to be back yet,' she observed, seeing no light from the cook's room. 'Are you waiting up for Jodie, or going to bed?'

'It depends upon whose bed I'm sleeping in.'

She looked round quickly. He wasn't joking. She could see it in the quiet intensity of his eyes, and she took a long shuddering breath. He'd given her two choices today and the only thing she knew for certain was that she didn't want to leave.

'There's mine,' she managed to say. 'If...if you want it?'

'Want it?' he said with a blinding smile. 'Kate, if you only knew how much.'

Slowly she led the way along to her bedroom and then turned to face him. And it was all right when he kissed her, teasing her lips gently apart with his tongue. And it was still all right when he undid the buttons of her dress and sent it pooling to the floor, before drawing her closer to him so she could feel the strength of his own arousal. It was when he slid her bra from her shoulders and cupped her bare breasts in his long lean fingers that something inside her turned to stone.

Maybe he won't notice, she prayed as he bent his head to take one of her nipples into his mouth and she felt nothing but dread. Maybe he won't care, she thought as he slipped his fingers down inside her briefs and she shuddered not with pleasure but with foreboding.

Every magazine she'd ever read had declared that men in the grip of desire didn't notice whether you were responsive or not, but unfortunately Ethan didn't seem to have read the same magazines. He drew back from her slightly, searched her face, then smiled a little ruefully. 'I'm not doing very well, am I?'

'No—I mean yes,' she corrected herself quickly. 'What you're doing, it's…it's wonderful.'

'Wonderful?' he echoed, his face suddenly sad. 'Don't you mean awful?'

'Ethan, it isn't you—please, don't think it's you,' she said swiftly. 'It's me. I want you—I do—but…'

'Tell me the truth, Kate,' he said, his eyes dark. 'Is it because I'm a CF carrier—is that why you don't want to get involved with me?'

'No—*no*!' she exclaimed, horrified that he would even think it. 'I don't carry the gene and I know if you and I…if we…if we had a baby it wouldn't have CF.'

'Then what is it?'

How could she explain what she didn't understand herself?

'I don't know,' she began hesitantly. 'I do want you, but—'

'You feel guilty, as though you were somehow cheating on Simon?' he said gently.

'Maybe—perhaps—I don't know. Ethan, w-what are you doing?' she stammered as he slipped her bra back over her shoulders and fastened it.

'It's too soon for you.'

'But you said—'

'Forget what I said.' He smiled, and his smile was a little crooked. 'I told you I was a patient man, and I lied. I want you very badly but it was wrong of me to pressurise you, and I won't do it again.'

'Ethan, I'm the one who should be apologising—'

'For loving your husband?' He shook his head. 'Don't ever apologise for that. Kate, listen to me,' he continued, gripping her tightly by the shoulders as she gazed at him, troubled. 'I don't want to take Simon's place or make you forget him. All I want—all I'm asking for—is for you to find a place in your heart for me.'

Tears welled in her eyes. 'I want that too—I do—but the trouble is, I don't know if I can.'

'Kate, love isn't something you can only give to one person and then have to take it away in order to give it to someone else,' he said gently. 'You can grow more love—a different love—if you really want to. And now I'd better go,' he added with an effort, running his thumb lightly across her lips, 'because I know if I stay here much longer I'm going to make love to you whether you want me to or not.'

And as he swung out of the door she stared after him and felt hot tears trickling slowly down her cheeks.

CHAPTER SEVEN

'WHY do I always miss all the excitement?' Jodie protested as she clapped her hands against her chest to release the trapped mucus in her lungs. 'First it was that kid down in Kitzbühel, and now this car crash. Everyone's talking about it—saying how you and Dad were the heroes of the hour—and I have to go and miss the whole thing!'

'There were moments in that operating theatre when I'd have been quite happy to have missed the whole thing,' Kate declared wryly. 'Hey, slow down,' she admonished, adjusting the angle of the tipping bed slightly as the girl rolled onto her other side. 'Physio isn't supposed to be something you finish in the fastest possible time, you know.'

'Yes, but—'

'Jodie, Herr Zimmerman and Franz haven't even arrived yet.'

The girl grinned ruefully as she huffed, coughed and spat into the beaker Kate was holding out to her.

'I'm just so looking forward to this trip,' she said fervently, beginning to clap her hands against her thin chest again. 'We're going to ride in one of those horse-drawn carriages, visit the Getreidegasse where Mozart was born, see the Mirabell Gardens—'

'Do Franz and his father know what they're letting themselves in for?' Kate interrupted with a chuckle.

'Of course!' Jodie replied, sticking out her tongue at Kate. 'It was Herr Zimmerman who planned the itinerary after I said I wanted to see as much of Salzburg as possible.'

'Just don't overdo things, OK?' Kate declared, gazing

critically down at the sputum in the bottom of the beaker.
'The infection you had back at Malden has cleared up really
well but we don't want it coming back again.'

Jodie nodded in agreement, then shot her a long, sidelong
glance from under her blond eyelashes.

'Speaking of Herr Zimmerman,' she began with studied
casualness, 'he's rather a handsome man, isn't he? I mean,
I know he's not young or anything,' she continued as Kate
binned the beaker and reached for a fresh one. 'In fact, he
must be every bit as old as my dad, but for someone in his
forties he's really well preserved, and he must be quite rich
if he owns all those hotels.'

'I guess so,' Kate murmured absently, jotting down a few
quick notes in her notebook. 'Huff, cough and spit for me
again, Jodie.'

Quickly the girl did as she asked, then levered herself
up onto her elbows. 'You like him, don't you?'

'Who?'

'Herr Zimmerman,' Jodie declared in clear exasperation.
'And I know he likes you. Franz says he's always talking
about you.'

'That's nice.' Kate smiled, carefully examining the second sample.

'And he thinks you're really nice—Herr Zimmerman,
that is,' Jodie continued doggedly. 'And personally I think
you could do a lot worse.'

'A lot worse than what?' Kate asked, puzzled.

'Marrying him.'

'*Marrying* him?' Kate exclaimed. 'Now, hold on a minute—'

'Think about it, Kate,' Jodie interrupted quickly. 'If you
married him you'd never want for anything, and you'd get
to live in Kitzbühel, which I know you love, and I could
come visit you and see Franz in the holidays—'

'Hey, just a minute,' Kate said, starting to laugh. 'Am I
marrying this man for my benefit or yours?'

'OK, I admit it would be really convenient for me.' Jodie grinned. 'But you should marry again, Kate, and doesn't it make sense to marry someone rich and good-looking?'

'It certainly does,' Kate said dryly. 'In fact, I can see only one tiny flaw in this grand plan of yours. I hardly know the man, and he doesn't know me.'

'That's easily remedied. I could tell him today that you'd love to go out with him—'

'And if you do I'll put you on a course of antibiotics administered the hard way,' Kate interrupted. 'I mean it, Jodie,' she continued firmly as the girl opened her mouth to protest. 'If I hear one whisper from Gunther that you've been arranging my social life, you'll need a cushion to sit down for a week.'

'OK, OK, I won't say anything,' the girl said with a sigh, 'but, like I said, I think you could do a lot worse.'

'I'm sure I could,' Kate replied, 'but I'd at least like to have some say in the matter. Hey, just a minute, young lady,' she said as Jodie rolled off the tipping bed and made for the veranda door. 'I haven't taken your temperature yet.'

'It's fine,' Jodie declared, quickly backing away from her.

'Developed ESP, have you? Come on, open your mouth.'

'You're such a fuss-budget,' the girl grumbled as Kate slipped the thermometer between her teeth. 'Between Dad clucking over me like a broody hen and you acting like a prison warden—'

'You have a dog's life,' Kate finished for her. 'Now keep the thermometer between your teeth and shut up for a minute.'

The girl subsided into a belligerent silence, and Kate chuckled inwardly. Of all things for Jodie to come up with, the idea of her marrying Gunther Zimmerman had to be the craziest. She scarcely knew the man, except as Franz's father, and handsome though he might be, rich though he undoubtedly was, she would never marry him in a thousand years.

'Is it OK?' Jodie demanded as Kate stared down at the thermometer.

'It's fine.'

'Told you,' Jodie declared cheekily. 'And they're here!' she added with a shriek of delight as they both saw a car coming up the road towards the chalet.

'Now, are you sure you've got everything?' Kate asked, quickly packing the last of the girl's drugs into a chill-bag. 'Sunscreen, sun-hat, spare shoes—'

'Why not just pack everything I own and be done with it?' Jodie interrupted in exasperation. 'I'm only going to Salzburg, for heaven's sake, not the far side of the moon!'

'Yes, but you're not exactly going to endear yourself to either Herr Zimmerman or Franz if you have to come back for anything. OK, I think that's everything.'

'Thank heaven for that,' Jodie exclaimed with feeling, making for the veranda door. 'I'll be fine—honestly I will. In fact, I'm more concerned about you and Dad. Aren't you going to be dreadfully bored stuck here in the chalet while I'm in Salzburg? Rhona's taking the car down to Kitzbühel to get the results of her tests and it could be hours before she gets back.'

'I'm sure your dad and I will find plenty to keep us busy,' Kate replied.

They would have to, she thought, following Jodie ruefully outside to find Ethan helping Gunther load a picnic basket into the car boot.

Since the night of the car crash Ethan had behaved impeccably. Not by a word or a look had he exerted any pressure on her, but it hadn't helped.

Just glancing up and finding his eyes on her, so warm and gentle, was enough to start her heart racing. If their hands accidentally touched, her stomach contracted into a hard, painful knot. Even simply sitting next to him in the car, sent her pulses into overdrive as her fingers ached to reach out and caress his jaw.

Time and time again she'd relived that moment in her bedroom when she'd frozen, and time and time again she'd found herself wishing he'd overridden her doubts and made love to her. It would have been the easy way out and she wanted the easy way out. Taking the initiative herself, as she knew she would have to before he would touch her again, that was the hard way because if she ran away again, she couldn't live with herself.

'Are you sure you have everything you need, sweet-heart?' Ethan asked as his daughter scrambled excitedly into the back of Gunther's car. 'Enzyme capsules to eat during meals, salt tablets—'

'And my sunblock, and a sun-hat. Honestly, Dad, you and Kate are the giddy limit!'

'Sorry,' he said sheepishly.

'Do not worry, Herr Flett.' Gunther beamed, resplendent in a pair of white shorts and matching T-shirt. 'Franz and I will take care of her and make sure she comes to no harm. I'm just sorry you could not come with us today, Katharina,' he continued, turning towards her with regret in his eyes. 'I'm sure you would have loved Salzburg.'

Kate was sure she would have loved it too, but Jodie had made it quite plain that she wanted to make this trip on her own and it was time the girl was given the opportunity to spread her wings.

'Perhaps some other time, Gunther,' she said evasively, all too aware that Jodie was watching her keenly through the car window.

'You keep on saying that,' he protested, 'but we never make a definite date.'

And we won't, she thought, smiling noncommittally back at him.

'Try and make sure Jodie doesn't overdo things,' Ethan

continued as Gunther got into his car. 'And don't let her skimp on lunch or forget to take her tablets—'

'Look, would it put your mind at rest if Herr Zimmerman arranged for an ambulance to follow me for the whole day?' Jodie exclaimed with vexation.

Ethan held up his hands and grinned. 'OK, OK—end of lecture. Have a good time.'

'We will,' Jodie declared, and as Gunther drove slowly down the drive she hung out of the window and shouted, 'Don't get up to anything exciting while I'm away, OK? And if you're going to save anybody's life, could you hang on until I get back?'

And with a blast from his horn, and a cheery wave, Gunther manoeuvred the car down the steep drive, and disappeared from sight.

'They've certainly got a good day for their trip,' Ethan observed, gazing up at the cloudless blue sky. 'Sunny but not too hot, and there's a slight breeze.'

'And they definitely won't starve.' Kate laughed. 'Rhona's packed enough snacks to feed an army.'

'So we just have to obey my daughter's instructions and not do anything too exciting while she's away.' He smiled down at her.

It had been the wrong thing to say, and they both knew it immediately. His eyes locked with hers, and try as she may she couldn't look away.

The slight breeze he'd remarked on was ruffling his hair as gently as any lover's fingers, teasing and stroking it across his forehead in long, slow, fluid movements, and Kate shivered although the day was warm.

It was so quiet now that everyone had gone. She could hear the gentle breeze singing softly through the pine trees, the cheerful call of a bird as it sang to its mate, but louder than that—much louder than that—was the sound of her own heart drumming in her ears.

'I...I suppose we'd better get on,' she managed to say,

her voice sounding odd, husky, to her own ears. 'I have notes to write up, and you...you said you were going to work on chapter six of your book.'

'Did I?'

His own voice was low, roughened, and unconsciously she ran her tongue along her upper lip to moisten it and saw his eyes flare.

'Y-your book,' she repeated hurriedly. 'You did say you wanted to work on it, didn't you? And my notes—they really are important. If I don't keep on top of them, don't get them written while I remember—'

'Kate, it's all right,' he interrupted softly. 'I promised I wouldn't touch you again unless you wanted me to, re-member?'

She clasped her hands together and found that her palms were damp. That was the trouble, she thought wretchedly. She did want him to touch her again. What she didn't know was whether she could deal with it or not.

'So we'd better get on with this work you've mentioned,' he continued with an effort. 'Or they'll be back before we know it.'

Please, let that be true, she thought as she walked jerkily back into the house. Please, let this be one of the shortest days of my life.

It wasn't. It was interminable.

For two hours she tried to avoid him. When she went into the kitchen and found him there she backed out again swiftly, saying she'd get her coffee later. When she met him in the hallway she deliberately avoided any eye con-tact. It was when she rushed to answer the phone only to stop dead when he appeared that Ethan began to laugh.

'Oh, Kate, this is impossible! I'll go mad if we spend the rest of the day like this. Why don't we go down to Kitzbühel and visit all those places Jodie thinks are *boring?*'

'Do you think we should?' she said hesitantly. 'I mean…going out together…?'

His lips quirked. 'It's a lot safer than staying here, believe me. The good burghers of Kitzbühel may be broad-minded but even they'd cut up rough if I attempted to make love to you in the street.'

She laughed shakily. 'OK, Kitzbühel it is, but how are we going to get there? Rhona has the car, remember, and it's a twenty-mile round trip on foot.'

He frowned, then his eyes lit up. 'Bicycles—there are a couple of bicycles in the storeroom—we could cycle down.'

Her lips twitched. 'Maybe I could, but what about you?'

'I used to cycle everywhere when I was a boy,' he protested.

'That would be during the Boer War, would it?' she asked slyly.

'Ha, ha, very funny.' He grinned. 'Come on, Kate, it'll be fun.'

'It won't be tomorrow when you can hardly walk,' she pointed out.

His eyebrows rose quizzically. 'Me? *Me* who can hardly walk? I'll have you know I must have walked hundreds of kilometres since we came to Austria in an attempt to keep my mind off you.'

'Really?' she said, momentarily diverted. 'Is that really why you went hiking?'

'You'd better believe it,' he replied, his grin broadening. 'It was either that or cold showers, and I'd already tried the cold showers back at Malden and found they didn't work.'

'Walking isn't the same as cycling, Ethan,' she said, fighting the mounting colour which had swept across her face at his admission. 'You use an entirely different set of muscles, and I ought to know. I used to cycle to work in London every day because it was much faster than driving.'

'You're just scared I'll beat you down, aren't you?' he said, his eyes dancing.

'Beat me?' she replied indignantly. 'No chance!'

'Prove it. Last one down to Kitzbühel buys lunch.'

'You're on,' she said laughingly as they headed for the storeroom. 'And I'm warning you—it had better be fun or I'm taking a taxi home.'

It was fun. Fun to shriek and mock one another's efforts. Fun to laugh and joke and to pretend, even for a short time, that they were nothing more than two friends who were on holiday.

'I won, I won!' she sang out as her bicycle just edged in front of Ethan's as they came into the town.

'Only because you cheated by not stopping at that "Halt" sign back there,' he protested.

'Nothing was coming,' she exclaimed defiantly.

'Lucky for you or I'd be scraping you off the road,' he retorted, 'OK, OK,' he added with a grin as she pulled a face at him. 'Lunch is on me—but first some sightseeing.'

He took her to the fifteenth-century parish church with its tall slender spire and mountain-style hanging roof, and had her choking with laughter as he regaled a party of smiling Japanese tourists with a totally fictitious account of its history.

They visited the Liebfrauenkirche and she stared, entranced, at the painting *Coronation of the Virgin* on the vaulting, only to burst out laughing when he sprang out from behind one of the pillars and surprised not her but a very large Austrian lady instead.

'You're going to get yourself arrested if you carry on like this!' she exclaimed as they ran from the church with the sound of the irate woman's cries ringing in their ears. 'What's got into you today?'

'I don't know,' he admitted. 'I only know that I want... This is going to sound so ridiculous, but today I want to forget who I am and what I am. I want to be the person I was years ago—the person who had no responsibilities, no worries, no cares. Does that sound insane?'

She smiled and shook her head. 'Not to me it doesn't. So, what are you going to do next? Knock on people's doors and run away? Or how about…?' She paused and her eyes sparkled. 'Why don't we buy a tube of superglue and put it on all the benches in Kitzbühel?'

'Oh, Kate, you're wonderful!' he exclaimed, whirling her round in his arms. 'Don't change—promise me you won't ever change!'

'I'll do my best.' She laughed, holding on to him breathlessly. 'Though if we get arrested I might have to promise to reform. They might not let me out if I don't.'

He threw back his head and laughed, but as he did so he unconsciously drew her closer and they both knew immediately that it had been a mistake.

'Oh, but I want you, Kate,' he murmured into her hair, wrapping his arms around her. 'Why do you have to look the way you do, feel the way you do?'

His voice was ragged, uneven, and a soft sigh came from her as his lips began to trace the outline of her jaw. What she was letting him do was madness—sheer madness—but as his tongue slid gently into her mouth she knew that she didn't want him to stop. She didn't ever want him to stop. She clasped her hands round his neck and eased herself closer to him and that was an even bigger mistake. All too unmistakably she could feel his body stirring and hardening against hers and her knees buckled with her own answering arousal.

'So much for me thinking the wrath of the burghers would be a sufficient deterrent,' he said, releasing her quickly and running his hands through his hair in a gesture that tore at her heart. 'I can't even keep my hands off you in public.'

'Lunch,' she said, her breathing as unsteady as his. 'You owe me lunch, remember?' she continued as he gazed at her blankly. 'Or are you the kind of man who welches on a bet?'

'No...no, of course not,' he answered with an effort. 'Where...where can we go? We're not exactly dressed for the Schloss Berghof, are we?'

'Then what about a restaurant?' she suggested. 'There must be one that wouldn't mind serving two distinctly disreputable-looking characters.'

'Who are you calling disreputable?' he protested. 'I'll have you know I'm a consultant surgeon who used to work in Harley Street.'

Her eyes swept over his faded blue shorts and equally faded green checked shirt. 'This is Versace's new summer collection, is it? The I-haven't-got-two-pennies-to-rub-together look?'

He burst out laughing. 'Kate Rendall, you're one in a million!'

'One in ten million, I'd say,' she retorted. 'And modest with it.'

He laughed again but as he tucked her arm through his and led her down the Vorderstadt she knew that a day would come when his needing and wanting would be so great he just wouldn't be able to stop. And what would she do then?

'This place looks OK, don't you think?' Ethan remarked as he stopped outside a smart-looking restaurant.

Kate shaded her eyes with her hands and peered through the window dubiously. 'It looks a bit posh to me.'

'Let's try it,' he insisted. 'They can only throw us out.'

They didn't. The proprietor's lips may have curled at Kate's sleeveless blouse and jeans, and he may have stared very hard at Ethan's shorts, but he guided them to one of the booths without a word.

The food was excellent, and as they both made a determined effort to talk about generalities the meal should have been enjoyable—but it wasn't.

A group of British women occupied the booth next to theirs, and though they were not visible their conversation was most certainly audible. There wasn't a town in Austria they hadn't visited, a delicacy they hadn't sampled or a souvenir they hadn't bought, and none of their comments about the country or its inhabitants were complimentary.

'Ignore them,' Kate said in an undertone, recognising the signs of an impending explosion on Ethan's face.

'Pretty well impossible, don't you think?' he replied, and her heart sank.

The last thing she wanted was him storming round to give those women a piece of his mind—and he'd do it, she knew he would.

'I think I might have a slice of that gateau,' she said brightly. 'It looks really—'

She never did finish what she'd been about to say. The chattering females behind them had become, if anything, even more vocal, but it wasn't the sound of their voices that suddenly made her bereft of speech. It was what—or rather who—they were talking about.

'Well, I have to say I was shocked when I saw her with Dr Flett and his daughter at the Schloss Berghof,' a singularly strident voice announced. 'I mean, my dears, taking his *nurse* out to dinner! As I said to Brian at the time, who will it be next—his cook?'

A tinkle of malicious laughter greeted that comment and Kate found her hands curling into quite unladylike claws in her lap.

The bitches! The stupid, stuck-up bitches! She wished she already had her gateau. It would have given her the greatest pleasure to have pushed it into one of their superior faces. But they weren't finished. There was worse to come.

'Well, *I* heard she wasn't just his daughter's nurse,' an unpleasant-sounding woman said with a titter. '*I* heard they were lovers!'

A gasp greeted that revelation and Kate's eyes flew to

Ethan's and then away again. How could they know about that night in the chalet, how could anyone know?

'Do you suppose he'll marry her?' someone asked curiously.

'Good heavens, no,' the unpleasant-sounding woman exclaimed. 'It might be different if she had some beauty and class but the poor dear quite obviously hasn't. I mean, did you *see* the dress she was wearing at the Schloss Berghof? It's obvious the poor man's been on his own for far too long and he's simply reduced to satisfying his urges with the hired help.'

Ethan got to his feet, his eyes blazing, and Kate grasped his hand tightly.

'Don't—please, please, don't make a scene,' she said hoarsely. 'Let's go… Please, let's just go.'

For a second he stared down at her, clearly torn, then nodded grimly and called for the bill.

She didn't know how she made it out of the restaurant. All she knew was that she had never felt so embarrassed in all her life.

That was why all those women had kept staring at her in the Schloss Berghof. They thought she was Ethan's lover, and the worst of it was that she might have been if she hadn't chickened out at the last minute.

A sob came from her at that thought and he'd obviously heard her because he caught hold of her arm.

'Kate, those women—'

'Not here…not here,' she gasped, throwing off his hand and beginning to walk on, only to stop as a young woman came rushing up to them.

'Herr Flett! It is Herr Flett—the English doctor, is it not?' she asked.

'Yes, I'm Dr Flett,' he replied absently, his eyes fixed on Kate.

'Johann, it *is* him,' the woman continued, turning quickly

and beckoning to a man across the street. 'It is the English doctor who saved our Wilhelm's life.'

'Please, I did nothing,' Ethan declared swiftly as the man took his hand in a bear-like grasp and Kate began to walk on. 'I have to go—'

'Did nothing, he says,' the woman marvelled, shaking her head in disbelief. 'Without him we would have no son, is that not so, Johann?'

'*Ja.*' He nodded vigorously. 'Herr Flett, you must let us repay you in some way—'

'That won't be necessary,' Ethan interrupted, trying to extricate himself from the man's strong grip as Kate disappeared round a corner. 'If the boy is well it's all the thanks I need.'

'*Nein, nein*, we must do more,' the woman declared. 'My husband, he has the men's clothes shop, and you must call him if you need a new suit or a jacket and there will be no charge. I have the telephone number here somewhere...' she continued, beginning to hunt through her capacious handbag.

'It's most generous of you,' Ethan replied, desperation creeping into his voice, 'but there is no need, and I really do have to go.'

'Here—here is our card—and I want you to know—'

'Thank you—thank you, you are most kind,' Ethan interrupted, snatching the card from the bemused woman's fingers before dashing off down the street with a muttered oath.

Johann Tauber shook his head as he watched him go. 'These foreigners, Gretchen, they are not—how you say— quite together in their heads.'

'Perhaps not,' his wife replied, 'but never forget, Johann, without that man who is not all together in the head we would have no Wilhelm.'

'That is true, my *liebling*.' Johann nodded, then sighed.

'But I cannot help but wish he might have been a little less strange.'

Kate had almost left the outskirts of Kitzbühel before Ethan caught up with her, and one look at her face told him there was no point in speaking to her right then. She was too hurt, too upset, to listen to anything he might have to say.

They cycled back to the chalet in total silence. There was no laughter now as they struggled up the steep hills. No shared amusement as they part walked, part cycled, their lungs bursting with the effort. All Kate wanted was to get back to the chalet as quickly as she could to hide in her room, preferably for the rest of her life.

But why should she hide? she asked herself. She'd done nothing wrong. It was all in the minds of those women. Ethan had been right when he'd said people believed what they wanted to believe. Nothing she said or did now would ever alter their opinion of her. They'd damned her, and damned she would stay.

She glanced across at Ethan. He was watching her gravely, his face troubled, his eyes anxious. He didn't deserve to be the butt of those women's sniggering jokes, their horrible innuendoes. He was a nice man, a kind man, and yet they damned him too. It wasn't fair, and it wasn't right, and suddenly she knew what she was going to do.

The minute they got back to the chalet she threw her bicycle to the ground and strode indoors, her face determined.

'Kate, those women—pay no attention to them,' he said as he followed her inside. 'They're ignorant and spiteful, with nothing to do with their time but gossip.'

She didn't say a word. She just kept on walking until she reached her bedroom. He came after her, his face concerned.

'Kate, say something—say anything,' he begged. 'Look, I'll go back—confront them—tell them if they continue spreading their malicious rumours I'll sue them for slander.'

For an answer she began pulling off her clothes. First her trousers, then her blouse.

'Kate…Kate, what the hell are you doing?' he demanded in confusion.

'What it looks like,' she retorted. 'I want you to make love to me.'

'*What!*' he exclaimed, stunned.

'You heard what those women down in the village said,' she continued furiously. 'Well, I might as well be damned for something I've actually done as something I haven't.'

'Kate, will you stop this?' he said, trying to stay her hands as she reached for the catch of her bra. 'You don't make love to someone out of anger—I sure as heck can't.'

'You could,' she blurted out before she could stop herself. 'I bet you could if you really tried.'

He stared at her, open-mouthed, for a second, then his shoulders began to shake and he began to laugh. 'Kate…oh, Kate…'

Crimson colour flooded her cheeks and to her dismay hot tears filled her eyes. 'Don't, Ethan, don't laugh at me—'

'I'm not laughing at you,' he interrupted, his voice a warm caress. 'I'm laughing at the irony of all this. I try to make love to you, using all the skill at my disposal, and you knock me back, and now because of what those women said…'

'You laugh at me,' she said wretchedly.

He shook his head. 'Kate, you may act like an idiot at times, but I wouldn't laugh at someone I love. Now, put your clothes back on.'

'You do, don't you?' she said with wonder, staying his hand as he attempted to ease her blouse over her arm. 'You really, truly love me?'

'What do I have to say to make you believe me?' he protested. 'Of course I love you, you wonderful idiot!'

And she suddenly realised what should have been blindingly obvious to her before. She loved him.

He'd been right when he'd said she'd felt guilty that night, as though she were somehow cheating on Simon. She had felt guilty, but Simon was dead and he wasn't ever going to come back, and it wasn't wrong to find happiness with someone else. What was wrong was denying it.

Tears began trickling slowly down her cheeks, but this time she didn't try to stop them and she didn't apologise.

'People—my friends—they kept saying, ''You're young—you'll find someone else,''' she said, her voice shaking. 'As though losing Simon was like losing a favourite piece of jewellery—'

'As though finding someone else as special again was the easiest thing in the world,' he said with a nod.

'I never thought it would happen,' she said, dashing a hand across her wet cheeks. 'I never thought I could possibly fall in love again, but…'

'But?' he prompted, his voice low, his eyes fixed on her.

'Ethan, I do love you,' she whispered. 'And I want very much for you to make love to me.'

'You're sure?' he said, scanning her face. 'Kate, please, be sure, because I don't know if I could stop this time.'

'I wouldn't want you to,' she murmured.

And to prove it she stretched up, pulled his head down to hers and kissed him.

For a moment he stood motionless, not touching her at all, and she could feel the hard bunching of the muscles in his shoulders as though he was keeping himself under tight control. But when she opened her mouth to his, when she gave a tiny sigh as he tentatively kissed her back, a low groan came from somewhere deep in the back of his throat and his arms came round her in a crushing embrace.

There was nothing tentative about his mouth now. His

lips were hot, urgent, demanding, and she surrendered completely. All she wanted was to touch him, to taste him, and her fingers were as urgent as his as they reached for each other's clothes.

Only when she was standing naked before him did he pause and draw back.

'Kate…' he began, then stopped. He clenched his hands together tightly and she saw they were trembling. 'Kate, I want you so much but I don't know…I don't know whether I can be slow or gentle about it.'

She gazed up into his blue eyes and her own vision blurred at the love and need she saw there. 'Just love me,' she said simply, holding out her arms to him.

And he did, his hands and lips teasing and caressing every inch of her until she couldn't think, could barely speak, could only feel.

'Ethan, please,' she gasped eventually into his chest, lifting her hips for him, longing for, needing, that final culmination, and when he entered her, and carried her with him to a shattering, pulsating climax, she buried her face in his neck and knew she had found the man she wanted to spend the rest of her life with.

CHAPTER EIGHT

'I DON'T see why I need to go back to Malden, Dr Flett,' Rhona protested. 'Just because I've got this mitral incompetence thing, it doesn't mean I have to go home.'

'You have to go home because I want you to rest, take things easy—'

'Dr Stollinger didn't say anything about resting or taking things easy,' the cook declared, her jaw setting squarely. 'In fact, he said if I remembered to take the pills he's given me to regulate my heartbeat, and some other pills to get rid of the excess fluid in my body, I would probably outlive him.'

'That's true, but—'

'I don't want to go home, Doctor,' she interrupted, 'and if you make me go I'll simply worry about Jodie all the time so I'd be far better off here.'

Ethan sighed deeply and gave in. 'All right, you can stay. But only on the understanding that you take things easier from now on,' he added as the cook's face lit up.

'Of course I'll take things easier.' She nodded. 'You can count on it.'

'I wouldn't.' Kate chuckled as Rhona left the sitting-room. 'Rhona's idea of taking things easy is baking one cake for Jodie's tea instead of two.'

'I know,' he said wryly. 'Which is why I think we should all go back to Malden. Travelling backwards and forwards every day to Kitzbühel to collect the shopping can't exactly be stress-free for Rhona, even though her command of German is very good.'

'Couldn't we do the shopping for her?' Kate suggested. 'I wouldn't mind.'

'Neither would I, but Rhona would simply start thinking we were worried about her and that would make her even more stressed.'

'I guess so,' she murmured with a small sigh.

'What's wrong?' He smiled, slipping his arm round her waist. 'Scared if we go back home I won't love you any more? That I'll decide what we shared was nothing more than a brief holiday romance?'

'Something like that,' she murmured, flushing slightly.

'No chance,' he declared. 'For good or ill, you're stuck with me, Kate Rendall.'

She chuckled and he kissed her, gently at first and then with increasing urgency and intensity.

'Ethan, don't,' she protested breathlessly, desperately trying to evade his warm mouth and extricate herself from hands which had somehow managed to slip up under her T-shirt and were purposefully searching for the catch of her bra. 'What if Rhona comes in—or Jodie?'

He swore softly and released her.

'Kate, do you know how long it is since I made love to you? Three days—three days and three long, miserable, lonely nights.'

'I know, but—'

'Let me tell them about us,' he pleaded. 'I hate all this sneaking around, grabbing kisses in corners like a couple of school kids, feeling guilty when we've done nothing to feel guilty about. Kate, I don't want to make love to you just once. I want to marry you, spend the rest of my life with you.'

'I want that, too, but Jodie—'

'She'll be thrilled to bits when she hears. She likes you, you know she does.'

'As her nurse, yes,' she argued, 'but, Ethan, we're talking a radical shift of relationships here. I'd be her step-mother—'

'And she'll adore having you as a stepmother every bit as much as I'm going to adore having you as a wife.'

Kate stared at him dubiously. She wasn't nearly so sure. Not once had Jodie ever hinted about the two of them getting together. She'd hinted enough about Gunther, but never about Ethan.

'Kate, we're going to have to tell her some time,' he continued, as though he'd read her mind.

'I agree,' she said. 'And maybe in a few weeks—'

'A few *weeks*!' he exclaimed in dismay. 'I was hoping we could tell her today or tomorrow.'

'We can't,' she said firmly. 'We have to get her used to the idea of us being together. Once we go back to Malden and you've taken me out a few times—'

'That settles it,' he announced. 'If I can't touch you until we go back to Malden I'm getting on that phone right now to book our tickets home on Friday.'

'What's the rush?' she teased, her eyes dancing. 'Everyone knows abstinence makes the heart grow fonder.'

'That's absence, woman, not abstinence,' he growled, 'and, I tell you this, if I have to put up with much more of this abstinence I'm going to go explode.'

'I'm not surprised, considering you had three croissants for breakfast,' Jodie commented as she swung into the study. 'I told you you'd be sorry. Hey, have I interrupted something?' she continued, gazing with a puzzled frown from Kate's slightly flushed cheeks to her father's much deeper colour.

'Of course not,' Kate managed to reply. 'Your father's just been telling me we'll be going back to Malden on Friday.'

'But that's only four days away!' Jodie declared in dismay. 'We can't go home so soon—I can't!'

'Sweetheart, we can't stay on here indefinitely,' Ethan said soothingly. 'There's your education to think of, for one thing, and if I'm going to return to work I'll need to start applying for jobs.'

Kate glanced across at him in surprise. 'You're serious? You're actually going back to work?'

He nodded. 'I thought I might ring St Margaret's in Newcastle when we get back—see if they'd be prepared to take me on part-time.'

'Oh, Ethan, I'm so pleased,' she said softly. 'You're making the right decision, I know you are.'

'Well, I'm glad somebody's pleased,' Jodie exclaimed tearfully, 'because I want you to know that you've just ruined my life!'

'Ruined her life?' Ethan said in confusion as his daughter banged out of the study. 'Does she mean she doesn't want me to go back to work?'

Kate sighed. 'Of course she doesn't. It's Franz. She thinks if we go home he's going to forget all about her, and she'll never meet anyone like him ever again, and she'll be doomed to live out the rest of her life alone and lonely in a garret.'

'A garret?' he repeated, even more bewildered. 'Since when did Malden become a garret?'

'Since never,' she said in exasperation. 'Ethan, she's fifteen years old and in love for the first time. You must remember what that felt like.'

For a moment he said nothing, then chuckled. 'Lord, yes. Her name was Lizzie Watkins and when she dumped me in favour of my best friend I was convinced my life was over. Even thought about entering a monastery, of all things. Look, would it help if I went and talked to her?' he said. 'Tell her there are plenty more fish in the sea and that Franz is a bit of a wet weekend anyway.'

'I think it might be better if I talked to her,' Kate said hurriedly, vividly aware of what Jodie's reaction would be if he told her that. 'Woman to woman, so to speak.'

'OK, but don't let her talk you into agreeing to stay on

here longer,' he said as she made for the door. 'No matter what unrequited feelings my daughter may have for the wonderful Franz, we're going home on Friday.'

'So, you see, it doesn't make a whole lot of sense, you staying on in Austria if Franz is going to be enrolling at London University in a couple of weeks' time, does it?' Kate said softly as Jodie wiped the tears from her face and blew her nose vigorously.

'I guess not.' She hiccuped. 'But, Kate, that girl we saw him with when we went up the Kitzbüheler Horn. She's going to London University too. I'm going to be stuck in the wilds of Northumberland and Marta will be able to see him every day.'

'Not unless she's taking civil engineering she won't,' Kate said.

'She isn't,' Jodie replied, brightening visibly. 'She's taking English literature.'

'Which means she won't see him in any classes, and I very much doubt if she'll be able to meet him for lunch because the campuses are far too far apart.'

Jodie digested that information.

'I could see him at weekends, couldn't I?' she said slowly. 'I could go down to London, or he could come up to Malden for a break.'

'Absolutely,' Kate said with a nod.

There was no point in telling Jodie that first loves were generally just that, and that once at university and surrounded by new friends it was doubtful whether Franz would even remember the English girl he'd met in Austria, far less want to make the long journey north. There would be time enough for Jodie to face that fact, and all Kate could do when they returned to Malden was to encourage her to meet other young people in the hope that it would ease the pain when she realised her holiday romance was over.

'Now, I want no more tears, Jodie, OK?' she continued, getting briskly to her feet. 'And while I'm here I may as well check your weight—I didn't do it before breakfast.'

With a sigh the girl stepped on the scales, and as Kate gazed down at it she frowned.

'Your weight's gone down.'

'It's probably because of all the tennis I've been playing.'

'Yes, but your temperature was up a little this morning, too.'

'Only by half a measly degree,' the girl protested.

'It might simply be half a measly degree but I'm going to start you on a course on antibiotics,' Kate said firmly. 'And I want you to give your tennis lessons a miss for a couple of days.'

'Oh, Kate, no!'

'You can still go down to Kitzbühel to watch Franz play,' she said as Jodie gazed at her anguish. 'I just don't want you playing, all right?'

Jodie scowled belligerently but there was no way Kate was going to be swayed. A small rise in temperature and a drop in weight could mean nothing, but it could also be the herald of something serious.

'Please, don't tell my dad about me being on antibiotics,' Jodie said quickly as Kate began sterilising the nebuliser pots. 'He'll fuss, and I can't bear being fussed over.'

'Jodie, I have to tell him.'

'Why? You said my temperature was only up a little and I've lost what—one kilo? We're not exactly talking anorexia, are we?'

No, we're not, but you're so painfully thin to start with that losing even one kilo isn't good, Kate thought with a sigh.

'Jodie, I don't like keeping things from him.'

'You didn't object when we kept quiet about me learning

to do my own physio,' the girl protested. 'In fact, you were the one who insisted I didn't say anything.'

'That was different,' Kate replied. 'I was supervising you all the time, making sure you didn't get into trouble. This is a symptom, Jodie. OK, it may mean nothing at all, and your temperature could well be back to normal tomorrow—'

'Then couldn't we wait until tomorrow—see what it is before we tell him? Kate, you know what he's like,' she continued in her best wheedling tone. 'He's the most awful fuss-budget, and I don't want him getting all uptight for nothing.'

Jodie was right. The least suspicion of a problem with his daughter's health and Ethan's panic button went on red alert.

'All right,' she said slowly, 'but if your temperature's still up tomorrow I'm definitely telling your father.'

'Everything OK?' Ethan asked when Kate came out of Jodie's bedroom some time later. 'Franz and everything, I mean?'

'For the moment,' she replied. 'The really hard part is going to be if he doesn't contact her when we get back to Malden, as I'm rather afraid he won't.'

'We'll cross that bridge when we come to it,' he said, following her along to the sitting-room. 'Oh, and I've told Rhona we'll do the shopping for her this morning,' he went on, 'so is Jodie about ready to leave for her lesson?'

Kate's heart sank. She'd assumed Rhona would be driving them down and Ethan need never know his daughter wasn't playing tennis, but now... Well, it wasn't her problem, she decided. She'd agreed not to tell Ethan about Jodie's rise in temperature but she most certainly hadn't agreed to lie for her. How Jodie got out of this was her own affair.

And she did get out of it. As soon as she learned her

father was accompanying them she smiled with apparent delight.

'Oh, that's great. Franz phoned me earlier to say our lesson's been cancelled for today. He's asked me to meet him for lunch at one o'clock instead so I can hang around with you guys until then.'

Ethan swallowed the story completely and Kate would undoubtedly have done so, too, if she hadn't remembered that the one phone in the chalet was in the sitting-room and Jodie had been nowhere near it all morning.

She waited until they were making their way out to the car and grasped Jodie firmly by the elbow. 'That's the last time I'll stand by and watch you lie to your father, young lady,' she muttered under her breath.

'It worked, didn't it?' Jodie replied with a cheeky grin, and Kate shook her head and sighed.

It had but there was no way she was going to countenance any more lies. If the girl's temperature had gone up by so much as half a degree by tomorrow morning she'd be informing Ethan.

The shopping didn't take long. In fact, the single potentially sticky moment was when Kate needed to go into the *apotheke* to buy some multivitamins and fortified milk. Ethan might not have realised that his daughter couldn't have received a phone call that morning but he would know instantly what the purchase of those items meant—that his daughter's weight had dropped.

Jodie solved the problem by dragging him into a nearby souvenir shop on the pretext of looking for a gift for Di, but try as she might she couldn't dissuade him from remaining in town until she met Franz for lunch.

'You're not wandering around the town on your own for the next two hours, Jodie,' he said, his face implacable.

'Oh, for heaven's sake, Dad, I'm not a little kid—'

'No, you're not,' he interrupted. 'You're a very pretty teenager, and that's what worries me. No discussion, no arguments, Jodie,' he continued as she opened her mouth to protest. 'We're staying with you until lunchtime, and that's that. Now, I, for one, would like a cup of coffee after all that shopping—how about you, Kate?'

She nodded and suppressed her laughter at the sight of Jodie's truculent expression as Ethan purposefully led the way towards one of the pavement cafés.

Wanting coffee, however, that was one thing. Actually getting it this morning, that was something else.

'I think it would be a whole lot quicker if I went inside and placed our order,' Ethan said with a frown after he'd attempted for the fourth time to catch the eye of one of the waitresses. 'Coffee suit you, too, Jodie?'

She nodded and Kate waited until Ethan was safely out of earshot before turning to her, her face stern.

'OK, I want the truth from you, and I want it now. How can you be meeting Franz for lunch when you and I both know he didn't phone you this morning?'

A faint wash of colour appeared on Jodie's pale cheeks and she had the grace to look uncomfortable. 'The whole gang from the tennis club always goes to the Mueller Café for lunch on a Monday. I've never been able to join them before so I thought I might just turn up—give them a surprise.'

'And if they're not there?' Kate demanded. 'What if for this particular Monday they decide to go somewhere else— what are you going to do then? Wander aimlessly about Kitzbühel, looking for them? Jodie, you know how important it is for you to eat at regular times,' she continued when the girl said nothing. 'You can't afford to skip a meal.'

'I could still have my lunch at the café even if they're not there,' she declared truculently.

'And afterwards, just how—exactly—do you propose to get home without Franz to drive you?'

'By taxi, of course,' she said.

'Do you have any idea how much that will cost?' Kate protested. 'Not to mention the cost of your meal. Eating out in cafés in Austria isn't cheap, you know.'

'What am I going to do?' Jodie said miserably. 'I can't tell Dad I lied to him—he'd never forgive me.'

Kate gazed at the girl's unhappy face and relented. 'OK, this is what we'll do. You stay with us until lunchtime and we'll take you to this café. If Franz and his friends aren't there you can say they left a message saying that they couldn't make it, and we'll take you home again.'

Jodie's face lit up. 'Kate, I was right about you being OK. You're more than OK—you're one of the best.'

Tell her, her mind whispered. You'll never have a better opportunity to tell her about your love for her father. Awkwardly she cleared her throat. 'Jodie—'

'That necklace you're wearing,' Jodie interrupted suddenly, leaning towards her with a slight frown. 'I've only just real-ised—it's one of the ones we saw at Herrenchiemsee, isn't it?'

Kate's hand flew nervously to the locket she'd put on without thinking that morning and she coloured slightly. 'Yes, yes, it is. Jodie, there's something I'd like to talk to you about—something really important—'

'I don't remember you buying it,' the girl said, her frown deepening. 'In fact, I thought you said they were too ex-pensive.'

Inwardly Kate cursed her own stupidity for not remem-bering Jodie's keen eye for detail but she managed to reply with scarcely a tremor, 'Your father bought it for me.'

'Dad—my dad bought it for you?' Jodie said in surprise. 'Why on earth did he do that?'

'I guess…I guess he realised how much I liked it,' Kate murmured, feeling herself reddening still further under Jodie's puzzled gaze.

'But—'

'Our coffees shouldn't be long now.' Ethan smiled as he

joined them. 'Apparently there are a couple of touring buses in town and that's why it's so busy.'

'I'm not surprised,' Kate said quickly. 'It's such a lovely place, and there's so much to see and to do, and…and the buildings are so pretty, and so…so typically Austrian.'

And I'm babbling, she thought, painfully conscious of Ethan's puzzled gaze but even more acutely aware of the frown that still creased Jodie's forehead.

And it was a frown that didn't disappear. When Ethan decided it would be pleasant simply to stroll around the old town after they'd had their coffees, instead of going anywhere specific, Jodie's gaze seemed to be on them constantly—and it was a gaze that became more and more uncertain and perturbed.

'She suspects something, Ethan,' Kate said as they drove back to the chalet after dropping Jodie off at the Mueller Café where thankfully Franz and his friends were lunching.

'I hope she does,' he replied. 'I'm tired of all this pussyfooting around, and I keep telling you she'll be over the moon when she hears.'

'I wish I had your confidence,' she sighed. 'I wanted to sink through the floor when she noticed my locket.'

'You really are a worry-wart, aren't you?' He grinned.

'A what?' she said, beginning to laugh.

'It's one of Di's favourite expressions,' he replied. 'Meaning you constantly make mountains out of molehills.'

Perhaps she did, but when they reached the chalet she still had the horrible feeling that this particular molehill was going to turn out to be one huge great mountain in reality.

'That's odd,' Ethan said with a slight frown as he unloaded their shopping from the car and the chalet door stayed firmly closed. 'Rhona's usually out here fussing in case we've bought the wrong things.'

'You don't think…?' she began, and paused. 'I mean, she seemed perfectly fit this morning, but…'

'Well, there's one way to find out,' he replied, leading the way indoors.

'There's a note,' Kate exclaimed, seeing an envelope pinned to the sitting-room door. Quickly she scanned it, then smiled. 'Crisis over. She's been asked out to lunch by the Thompson family—the couple who've taken the chalet just down from us—because we're leaving on Friday, and she's left our lunch in the fridge.'

'Which means…'

'Means what?' she queried.

'That we have the whole house to ourselves,' he murmured.

There was no mistaking the message in his eyes and she shook her head quickly.

'Ethan, we can't. Rhona could come back at any time. And Jodie—we don't know when she'll be back, and…'

She stopped. He was holding out his hand to her, a warm smile curving his lips, and she could no more have ignored the entreaty in his eyes than flown.

'All right,' she said a little breathlessly, her heart already racing as he began leading her towards her room, 'but we'll have to be quick.'

He swore softly, then swung her into his arms and rested his chin on her forehead with a sigh.

'Kate, once—just once—I'd like to make love to you slowly. Once—just once—I'd like to go to bed with you at night and wake up with you there beside me in the morning.'

'I know, I know,' she whispered into his broad chest. 'And it will happen one day, but—'

'This time we have to be quick,' he finished for her with a grimace.

But he wasn't quick. Once their clothes had been shed haste was forgotten as he delighted in touching and tasting her with a tantalising tenderness that had her forgetting everything except her own spiralling need for him to bury himself deep within her and end this exquisite torture.

Had it ever been this good with Simon? she wondered as her whole body shuddered under the gentle onslaught of his hands and mouth. Had he ever made her feel quite so alive, and desired, and cherished?

She could remember moments when it had been almost as good but no one had ever made her feel so fulfilled as Ethan. No one had ever made her feel so completely whole so that when they were finally one, when he finally possessed her, and they journeyed together to a shattering climax she knew it was not simply a joining of bodies, but a joining of hearts and souls as well.

'OK?' he murmured huskily into her ear when her thudding heart finally began to return to normal.

'Wonderful,' she whispered truthfully, and heard him chuckle. 'How about you?'

One dark eyebrow rose. 'Do you have to ask?'

She laughed and ran her hands lightly down his back, feeling the faint slick of sweat in the hollow between his shoulders. Gently she stroked the dark hairs on his chest, brushing her fingers over the curled nubs of his tiny nipples, and heard him groan.

'Don't do that,' he murmured into her hair, his voice thick.

'I thought you liked it when I touched you?' she said in surprise.

'That's the trouble, as you can see—or rather feel,' he gasped, guiding her hand slowly downwards.

'Oh,' she said faintly, a rush of colour sweeping across her cheeks.

'Exactly,' he said wryly, resting his forehead against hers, 'so if you want to have any hope of getting out of this bed before everyone gets back—'

The rest of what he'd been about to say died in his throat as they both heard the sound of the chalet door clattering open, and when it was followed by the sound of light, running feet their eyes met in panic.

Swiftly Ethan reached for his trousers, but he was too late. Kate's bedroom door swung open and Jodie stood there, a look of distress on her face—distress that quickly turned to horror.

'Jodie, I can explain,' her father began. 'It's not what you think—'

'Oh, but it is,' she cried. 'It's exactly what I think. How could you—how *could* you?'

'Jodie, listen to me,' her father pleaded, wriggling out from under the bedclothes as Kate desperately tried to keep herself covered. 'I didn't want you to find out like this—I would have given anything in the world for you not to find out like this—but Kate and I, we love one another—'

'What you've been doing isn't love, it's just sex,' she flared. 'And to be doing it at your age—it's gross, it's disgusting!'

'Jodie—'

'How could you betray my mother like this? I'll never forgive you—never!'

And she turned on her heel and fled.

'Ethan, don't go after her just yet,' Kate said, scrambling out of bed after him as he dragged on his shirt and made for the door. 'Give her time to calm down, time to—'

But he wasn't even listening to her. Without a word he banged out of the bedroom and she heard the sound of his voice urgently calling to his daughter.

Quickly she reached for her own clothes, and as she pulled her sweater over her head she realised she was crying soundlessly. Just seconds ago she had felt so happy, so whole, and now, after seeing the look on Jodie's face, all she felt was sordid, cheap.

And it was her own fault. If she'd let Ethan tell his daughter what they felt for one another none of this would have happened.

She had scarcely finished dressing when Ethan came back, white-faced and tight-lipped.

'What happened?' she asked hesitantly.

'She won't talk to me,' he said grimly. 'In fact, she said she was never going to talk to me ever again.'

'Ethan, she didn't mean it,' she said, stretching out a hand to him, then letting it fall. 'She's upset. Maybe if I spoke to her—tried to explain how we feel…'

He shook his head. 'I don't think that's a very good idea.'

'Surely it's worth a try,' she argued. 'Where is she?'

'In her room, but, Kate—'

'Please,' she begged. 'It's as much my fault—if fault there is—as yours, and perhaps I can make her understand.'

She couldn't. Jodie was lying face down in the middle of her bed, her frail shoulders shuddering with sobs, but the moment Kate spoke her name she spun round, her eyes burning with hate. 'Get out! I didn't invite you in here, and I want you to get out!'

Her breathing was much too wheezy and there was a trace of white spittle on her lips. Kate took a step forward determinedly.

'I'm not going anywhere until we talk.'

'About what?' the girl threw back at her. 'About how you and my dad have been doing *that* for heaven knows how long?'

Kate whitened, but she'd come this far and she wasn't going to back down now.

'Jodie, I want you to listen to me. Your father and I have only made love twice—'

'*Love?*' the girl spat out, swinging her feet onto the floor. 'What you were doing with my dad wasn't *love*!'

'Jodie, no matter what you think—no matter what impression you may have gained—we do love one another, and he's asked me to marry him,' Kate declared with a calmness she was very far from feeling.

'He doesn't love you—he can't,' Jodie cried, dashing an angry hand across her wet cheeks. 'You're skinny and you're ugly and old. My mother was beautiful—everybody said so. If he's asked you to marry him it's because he wants an unpaid nurse for me.'

'Jodie—'

'And he's picked you because he knows he couldn't possibly ever fall in love with you—couldn't ever be disloyal to Mum. He loved my mother, he couldn't ever love you.'

'Jodie, listen to me—'

'So you can tell me more lies?' the girl hurled at her. 'No wonder you were so keen for me to go to design college. You wanted to get me out of the way, didn't you? Well, you can stuff your design college—I wouldn't go to design college if you paid me!'

'Jodie—'

'I thought you were my friend,' she said, her lips trembling. 'I thought I could trust you, but you weren't interested in me—you were only interested in my dad because he's rich and you've got nothing.'

'Jodie, that isn't true—'

'It is, I know it is. Now get out. Just…just get out!'

There was no point in staying. It was obvious Jodie was in no mood to listen to anything.

Ethan was waiting for her out in the corridor, his face as white and drawn as she knew hers must be.

'I gather it didn't go well?' he said, his voice ragged, rough.

'That's probably the understatement of the year,' she replied with an attempt at a smile that didn't work. 'Oh, Ethan, what are we going to do?'

'She'll come round,' he said firmly. 'It's…it's just been a bit of a shock for her to realise that her father's a man, too.'

'I guess so,' she said with a slight catch in her voice, and he put his arms round her and hugged her fiercely.

'Kate, she will come round,' he repeated. 'She *must*.'

She nodded, and tried to smile again, and to ignore the cold, bleak chill that seemed to have crept around her heart.

CHAPTER NINE

'I DON'T think you should go down to Kitzbühel this morning, Jodie.'

'Well, tough!' the girl exclaimed, tossing her blond hair back from her shoulders defiantly. 'Nobody asked you for your opinion.'

Kate gritted her teeth and struggled to remain calm. 'Your temperature's still up, and I told you yesterday—'

'I know what you told me, but you can save your breath. I'm going down to Kitzbühel to see Franz play and then he's taking me out to lunch. It's a date. You remember what those are, don't you?' Jodie continued, her lips curving into a sneer. 'Or maybe you don't go out on dates with men. Maybe you just sleep with them.'

Kate whitened then reddened in quick succession, and decided that enough was enough.

'Any more of that kind of talk, young lady,' she exclaimed tightly, 'and you'll be grounded for the rest of the week.'

'Says who?' Jodie jeered. 'You're not my mother—you never will be my mother. You're nothing but the hired help, the paid nurse, and my father could pick up a dozen like you simply by lifting the phone.'

'Jodie—'

'So you can stop giving me orders, Mrs Rendall. The only person who can do that is my dad and he says I can go.'

'He won't say that when I tell him about your temperature,' Kate said, making for the door grimly.

'He already knows,' Jodie declared, her face triumphant. 'I told him this morning.'

Kate didn't believe her, not for a minute, but prolonging the argument would do no good. She was getting nowhere as it was.

With as much dignity as she could manage she walked out of Jodie's bedroom and along to the study.

'What's wrong now?' Ethan asked, leaning wearily back from his desk when he saw her.

'Jodie says you've given her permission to go down to Kitzbühel,' she said without preamble.

'That's right.'

'Ethan, her temperature's up.'

'I know. She says it's because she's upset about us.'

Kate shook her head. 'It's more than that, I'm sure it is. Her weight's down, too.'

'By how much?' he asked, suddenly alert.

'Just one kilo,' she admitted, 'but—'

'Kate, she's really unhappy right now and if seeing this boy makes her smile again then surely the trip to Kitzbühel's worth it,' he interrupted. 'And it's not as though she'll be playing any tennis. I've put my foot down about that.'

She wanted to believe he was doing the right thing—part of her did believe he was doing the right thing—and yet still she could not rid herself of a nagging doubt.

'Kate, are you all right?' he asked, scanning her face anxiously.

She wasn't all right. She doubted whether she'd ever be all right ever again, and a small betraying sob broke from her despite all her best efforts to contain it. 'Oh, Ethan, why does everything have to be such a wretched mess?'

He was at her side in an instant, gathering her into his arms and holding her tight. 'It will come right, Kate. I *know* it will.'

'Will it?' she mumbled into the folds of his shirt.

'Give her time—that's what you told me, wasn't it?' he said as he gently stroked her hair, his face taut and strained.

'Once she's had time to think calmly and rationally, she'll understand.'

Privately Kate very much doubted it but she had no time to voice her doubts. The sharp sound of a car horn split the air and Ethan released her reluctantly. 'That's my taxi. The airline authorities want to see me in Innsbruck to finalise the arrangements for carrying Jodie's compressor and oxygen cylinders on Friday.'

'You're not taking Jodie down to Kitzbühel yourself, then?' she said, following him to the door.

He shook his head. 'She's taking a taxi. Look, why don't you come with me to Innsbruck?' he continued as she gazed at him uncertainly. 'I could be hours at the airport and I don't like to think of you here on your own, brooding.'

She was tempted—Lord, how she was tempted—but things were bad enough between them and Jodie, without the girl returning from town to discover they'd gone off together no matter how legitimate the reason.

'Don't be silly,' she said, forcing her lips into a smile. 'I'll be fine, and I won't be on my own. Rhona's here, remember.'

She was but, as Kate very quickly discovered, the cook's company was worse than no company at all.

How much Rhona knew of what had happened was anybody's guess, but she was either feeling singularly uncommunicative today or Jodie had given her a graphic account of what she'd walked in on and she didn't approve.

Every question Kate asked was answered by monosyllables, every comment largely ignored. Eventually she went out for a walk only to discover she could scarcely see the scenery through the blur of her tears. And there was no respite when Jodie came back. She exchanged a few brief words with Rhona then went straight to her room and slammed the door.

Kate stuck it out for as long as she could but eventually

her curiosity got the better of her and she went in search of Rhona.

'Did she have a good time—Jodie, I mean?' Kate asked, despising herself for being so craven as to pump the cook for information but knowing it was the only way she was going to get any.

'Hard to tell really. I think she might have overdone the tennis a bit. She looks really tired.'

'She played tennis this morning?' Kate exclaimed, only just biting down her anger at the news.

'Two sets apparently. Then stuffed herself silly at some café afterwards, which is probably why she's feeling a bit sick now.'

Kate was already out of the sitting-room, not knowing whether she wanted to strangle Jodie or comfort her. Of all the irresponsible things the girl could have done, playing two sets of tennis when she was on antibiotics had to be the worst. It would do nothing to lower her temperature and she wouldn't be at all surprised if it had gone up even more.

Determinedly she knocked on the bedroom door but when there was no reply she opened it to find Jodie lying sprawled on her bed, hunched over a book.

'I hear you're feeling a bit sick?' she commented.

Jodie's head came round briefly. 'Too right I'm sick—sick to my stomach at the way you and my dad have been behaving.'

There was more to it than that, much more. Even from the doorway Kate could see a fine sheen of perspiration on the girl's forehead, and her breathing was far too laboured.

'What you need is a glass of warm milk and honey to settle your stomach,' she said, turning to go.

'What I need is to see the back of you,' Jodie wheezed, 'and you know what you can do with your milk and honey!'

Without a word Kate made her way along to the kitchen

and poured some milk into a pan. The girl could call her every name under the sun, but somehow she was going to get the milk and honey down her throat even if she had to force-feed her.

She was halfway back down the hall when she heard it—the sound she'd hoped never to hear, the sound of Jodie gasping and choking for breath. With a smothered cry Kate banged the glass of milk down on a side table and flew into Jodie's room.

The girl's face was almost blue, her breathing was coming in great shuddering, rasping gasps and she was coughing up blood.

'Don't try to talk, sweetheart,' she ordered as she swiftly rolled the oxygen cylinder over to the bed and slipped the mask over the girl's head. 'Just breathe as slowly as you can. Slowly, Jodie—slowly!'

It was like telling a man who was dying of thirst not to drink. Fear was written all over Jodie's pinched features, fear and pain and dread.

Kate raced to the door and shouted as loudly as she could for Rhona. They had to get the girl to the nearest hospital, but where was it?

Innsbruck. She remembered Ethan telling her there were two hospitals in Innsbruck. Oh, Ethan, she thought frantically, why did you have to go away just now? Why couldn't you be here when we need you the most?

Rhona was at her side in seconds. 'What is it? What's wrong?'

'We need an ambulance. *Now*, Rhona!' she yelled as the woman gazed in horror at Jodie's face. 'We need one *now*!'

The ambulance came quickly but the journey to Innsbruck was a nightmare. Rhona had wanted to come with them but Kate had insisted she stay at the chalet and attempt to contact Ethan. In retrospect it had been a mistake.

She hadn't expected the paramedics' command of

English to be quite so limited, but when they arrived at the A and E department and she discovered that no one there appeared to be able to speak much English either, real fear clutched at her heart.

'There must be somebody!' she exclaimed as the receptionist gazed blankly at her. '*Wo gibt einen Art es*—oh, that's not right. *Wo gibt es einen Arzt, der Englisch spricht?*'

The receptionist reached for her phone and Kate prayed she was phoning for an English-speaking doctor and not for Security to have her thrown out.

Why, oh, why had they ever come to Austria? she wondered, wretchedly hearing Jodie's breathing become more and more laboured by the second. They should have stayed at Malden. If they'd stayed at Malden this might never have happened.

'I am Dr Kaufmann, *fraülein*,' a deep male voice suddenly said behind her. 'I understand you are needing help?'

Kate turned to see a young man with prematurely grey hair regarding her kindly. She could have kissed him.

'I'm Kate Rendall, and this is Jodie—Jodie Flett. She's fifteen years old, she has cystic fibrosis, her temperature's forty-two, and her sputum's bloody.'

She didn't have to say any more. Within seconds a team of white-clad medics had materialised and they were being rushed down a corridor.

'It looks to me like either pneumonia or an abscess,' Dr Kaufmann said when they came to a halt outside some double doors. 'We'll know more when we've done some tests, but the most important thing right now is to get her into isolation.'

'Can I come with you?' Kate begged. 'I'm a trained nurse—'

'Are you her mother?'

'No, but—'

'A member of the family?'

'No, but—'

'I'm sorry, *fraülein*,' Dr Kaufmann said gently but firmly. 'Only family are allowed into the isolation ward. If you go into the waiting room you will be able to see everything we do through the observation window.'

Wretchedly Kate turned to go, but before she could move Jodie had pulled the oxygen mask from her face and grasped her hand convulsively.

'Dad—where's my dad?'

'He'll be here soon, I promise,' she replied, clasping the girl's thin fingers tightly in her own. 'Rhona is trying to contact him, and I'm sure he'll be here any minute.'

'I don't want him any minute—I want him *now*,' Jodie insisted, her breath coming in great ragged gasps. 'Why isn't he here? He would be here if it wasn't for you—it's all your fault!'

'Jodie, listen to me—'

'*Fraülein*, we must go now,' Dr Kaufmann interrupted, gazing down at Jodie with concern, and before Kate could protest Jodie's hand was pulled from her grasp, the trolley was rapidly wheeled into the isolation ward and the doors were slammed shut.

Never had Kate felt so useless as she watched the medics take a sample of arterial blood from Jodie's arm to see how much oxygen her lungs were getting, then quickly link her to a heart monitor. She wanted to be in there, taking the Ventipuncture to check on Jodie's white blood cell count, or even doing something as simple as giving her water and sodium chloride to rehydrate her, not just standing out here, waiting.

Dimly she heard the sound of a commotion outside but ignored it. Her eyes were concentrated on the frail figure lying so quietly on the trolley and the medics who surrounded her. She didn't hear the waiting-room door open but she certainly heard the muttered oath behind her and her heart soared with relief.

'Ethan—oh, Ethan, thank God you've come!'

He didn't even acknowledge her presence. He just strode past her to the glass partition and stared at his daughter, his face haggard, his clothes dishevelled.

'I've killed her, haven't I?' he said hoarsely. 'I've killed her.'

'No, Ethan, no!' she exclaimed. 'She's very ill—'

'And she's going to die because of me,' he interrupted. 'You told me she wasn't well—you told me you were worried about her. If only I'd listened to you, if I hadn't been so arrogant—'

'Ethan, it wasn't arrogance. She was unhappy, upset, and you wanted to make her happy. You couldn't have foreseen—' She came to a halt as Dr Kaufmann appeared at the waiting-room door and went across to Ethan quickly. 'Is…is there any news? Jodie's samples—are they back from the lab yet?'

He didn't answer. Instead, his gaze raked Ethan with distaste and when he finally spoke his voice was ice-cold. 'I don't know who you are, but you'd better leave before I call Security.'

'This is Jodie's father, Dr Kaufmann,' Kate said hurriedly, seeing Ethan's back stiffen. 'Dr Ethan Flett.'

'He is also the man who created a disturbance in Reception,' Dr Kaufmann said, his lips a thin, tight line.

'I couldn't get them to believe I was Jodie's father,' Ethan muttered, his cheeks flushing.

'And you thought threatening to throttle our receptionist was the way to convince them?'

Ethan's colour darkened to crimson. 'I will apologise to the lady in question later, but right now I'm more concerned about my daughter. How is she?'

Dr Kaufmann's expression softened a fraction. 'Not good. Her blood tests show she definitely has a streptococcal infection and the carbon dioxide in her blood is much too high. We'll keep her on oxygen, pump her full of antibiotics, monitor her blood gases and watch the white blood cell count, but…'

'But?' Ethan demanded.

'She is not a well girl, Dr Flett. We will do what we can, but…'

The muscle in Ethan's jaw quivered. 'Can…can I see her?'

'Not yet. We must start her on a course of very strong antibiotics first and then you will be able to see her, but only for a few minutes. And you will have to wear a gown and a mask—we can't run the risk of her catching a further infection.'

Ethan nodded.

'I'm afraid it will probably be some time before we know whether your daughter will make a full recovery or not,' Dr Kaufmann continued. 'The hospital can supply you with food and basic washing facilities, but we have no accommodation other than this waiting room.'

'It doesn't matter,' Ethan said, his face strained. 'I won't sleep anyway.'

'And you, *fraülein*?' Dr Kaufmann asked, turning to her. 'Do you wish to stay also?'

Kate nodded. 'Yes, yes, I'm staying.'

A silence fell in the waiting room when Dr Kaufmann left, a silence that was broken only by the steady tick of the clock on the whitewashed walls. Then Ethan drew an uneven breath.

'Kate, do you think these people know what they're doing?'

'Their technique seems excellent—'

'I don't give a damn about their technique,' he flared, stabbing his hands through his hair desperately. 'Do you think I should try to get seats on a plane home—have her treated there?'

She doubted whether Jodie would survive the journey but she couldn't tell him that, she just couldn't.

'They know what they're doing, Ethan,' she said gently. 'They might not speak much English, but they do know what they're doing.'

He stared down at his hands and she saw the slight tremor at the side of his throat as he swallowed.

'What am I going to do if I lose her, Kate? If I lose her, I've got nothing, no one.'

Her heart twisted inside her. She wanted to say, you've got me, you'll always have me, but the words wouldn't come.

'She's a fighter,' she said with difficulty. 'She won't give up.'

He put the palms of his hands flat against the glass partition separating them from the isolation ward and closed his eyes.

'She's so small, Kate, so frail. How many more of these attacks can her heart take?'

'Ethan—'

'If I could only do something—anything,' he exclaimed, tears glittering under his closed lids. 'If they wanted an arm, or a leg, I'd give it willingly. If they asked for my whole damn life they could have it, but I can't *do* anything!'

She put her arms around him and held him tightly. 'She'll get better, Ethan. I just know she will.'

She doubted whether he even heard her. He had opened his eyes and was gazing at Jodie, his face etched with lines of despair.

'Ever since she was born I've thought, Why her? When I've seen other parents with their kids, maybe fighting, arguing, I've wanted to go up to them and say, don't you know how damn lucky you are? You're not living on a knife-edge, as I am, dreading the next infection.'

'Ethan—'

'She's frightened of the dark—did you know that?' he said hoarsely. 'I only managed to persuade her to get rid of her night-light a couple of years ago and now...when I think of her dying...' His voice cracked and she held him tighter. 'Kate, she'll be all alone in the dark with no one to cuddle her, no one to hold her, no one to tell her she's safe.'

Tears welled in her eyes and she cradled his head against her chest, only to release him as a nurse put her head round the waiting-room door.

'*Bitte*, Herr Flett. We have started your daughter on her antibiotics so you may see her for a few minutes if you wish.'

He went without a backward glance and Kate leant her head against the glass partition, her throat so tight she could hardly breathe. Please, get well, Jodie, she prayed as scalding tears trickled down her cheeks and into her mouth. Please, get well because I don't think either of us will survive if you don't.

The days and nights that followed seemed endless.

The staff at the hospital were very kind. They brought them coffee in little plastic beakers that tasted of nothing but which helped to pass the time. They brought them magazines to read and sandwiches to eat, but both lay largely untouched as their eyes strayed constantly back to the isolation ward where Jodie lay, unmoving, surrounded by a battery of machines.

Rhona came to visit but Ethan sent her away with instructions that she wasn't to come again after she'd burst into tears and couldn't be consoled. And to Kate's surprise Gunther arrived early one morning.

'I would have come before, Katharina,' he replied, kissing her hand gently, then sitting down beside her, 'but I did not want to be the intruder.'

'Of course you wouldn't have been intruding,' she insisted. 'I'm just sorry Dr Flett isn't here. He's gone to wash and shave but he will be back any minute.'

'It does not matter,' he replied. 'I came only to see how the little girl is, and to apologise for my son.'

'Apologise?' she said in confusion. 'Why should you need to apologise for him?'

To her surprise the normally unflappable Gunther looked acutely embarrassed. 'He should be here, himself, but…'

'He wouldn't come.'

It wasn't a question, but a statement, and Gunther nodded.

'He has never had to face the possibility of the death of someone so near to him in age before and I think it frightens him to realise he is mortal, too.'

'I understand,' Kate murmured, and wondered if Jodie would.

'He also feels responsible for Jodie's illness,' Gunther continued. 'Apparently they had the big fight about his friendship with Marta Schieber, and Franz with the callousness of youth told her he regarded her only as a little sister.'

'When did this happen?' Kate asked, frowning slightly.

'The day before she was taken ill. Franz tried to talk to her the next day, to soften what he had said, but he only made things worse. They had an even bigger fight so now you see why my son feels responsible.'

She could see, and now she knew why Jodie had looked so stricken that afternoon when she'd walked in on them and why she'd been so anxious to go down to Kitzbühel the next day.

'Please, tell him he is not to blame,' she said softly. 'Jodie's infection—I don't think any of us will ever know what triggered it.'

Relief appeared in his grey eyes and he reached out and took her hand in his. 'And what about you, Katharina? How are you? You look so tired.'

'I am tired,' she admitted. Not just physically exhausted, but mentally exhausted, too.

Each night when she curled up on one of the couches in the waiting room her body ached for sleep but her mind wouldn't allow it. Her mind kept returning over and over again to the yawning gulf which somehow seemed to have formed between her and Ethan.

She'd thought Jodie's illness would have drawn them closer together, that they would have taken comfort from each other's presence, but he scarcely spoke to her, barely even acknowledged her presence. Time and again she felt as though he was deliberately shutting her out and she didn't know why.

'Katharina?'

'I'm sorry, Gunther, what did you say?' she said with an effort, seeing the expectant look on his face.

'Only that if— I mean when the little girl gets better,' he corrected himself quickly, 'you will be returning to England, I think?'

She nodded, thanking Gunther silently for his tact. 'Her father will be anxious to take her home.'

'And you—you are anxious to go home, too?'

Just a few short days ago she would have been. Just a few short days ago she and Ethan had planned to gently introduce Jodie to the idea of them being a couple, but now…

'You do not have to go home, Katharina,' he said, his grey eyes fixed on her. 'You could stay on in Kitzbühel.'

She could not help but smile. 'Even if I wanted to, I couldn't. Who would employ me when I speak so little German?'

'I was not thinking of you working here,' he said softly. 'I was thinking—hoping—that you might stay on for a more personal reason.'

He was still holding her hand and she stirred uncomfortably in her seat.

'Katharina, I do not wish to embarrass you,' he said

quickly. 'I know all you feel for me is perhaps a friendship, but friendship could be a start, no?'

He was right. Out of friendship a kind of love might grow, and once perhaps it might have been enough for her. Perhaps once she would even have preferred it to a passionate love, but that had been before she'd met Ethan.

'Gunther, I'm sorry,' she began awkwardly, 'but—'

'You were not happy, I think, when you first came to my country,' he interrupted. 'But you have been happy here, yes?'

She thought back over the weeks she'd spent in Austria. Yes, she'd been happy, but she'd been happy because of Ethan and Jodie.

'Gunther—'

'It is all right, Katharina,' he said, patting her hand gently. 'I have seen the way you look at Herr Flett, but if things do not work out, if you ever find you need a friend, you will come to Austria, please?'

'I will come to Austria.' She nodded.

'And now I must go,' he said, getting to his feet.

'Won't you please stay until Dr Flett gets back?' she asked. 'I'm sure he'll be pleased to see you.'

He smiled for the first time since he'd arrived and shook his head. 'I think not. I have never been—how you say in English—the essence of the month with him.'

She also smiled but when he'd left her smile faded. Gunther had said that if things didn't work out between her and Ethan she was to come to him. Once—oh, it seemed a lifetime ago now—she would have had no doubts that she and Ethan would get married, but now... Now she didn't know what he was even thinking, far less feeling.

'Was that Gunther Zimmerman I saw in the corridor?' Ethan asked as he came into the waiting room.

She nodded. 'He came to see how Jodie was.'

'That was kind of him,' he said, throwing his jacket over a chair and going to the observation window.

'He's a very kind man. Ethan—'

'Has Dr Kaufmann been in yet?' he interrupted.

She shook her head. Each day they waited for him to deliver his daily bulletin, and every day it was the same. 'No change, no change.'

Awkwardly she got to her feet and went over to him. 'Ethan, I think we need to talk.'

'Talk?' he echoed. 'About what?'

'Us—we need to talk about us. Ethan, you're shutting me out,' she continued quickly as he turned his head away, hiding his expression. 'I thought we were a couple—'

'We are.'

'Then talk to me,' she insisted. 'I love Jodie, too, remember. I care about what happens to her as well.'

'I know you do,' he said, his eyes fixed on his daughter, his voice low.

'Then what's wrong?' she demanded. 'Times like these are supposed to draw people closer together, not force them apart, and that's what I feel is happening to us. Do you still feel responsible for her illness—is that it?'

'I will always feel responsible,' he murmured, his shoulders hunched in a manner so reminiscent of his daughter that she could have wept. 'I should have listened to you, and then for Jodie to walk in on us…'

'Ethan, that didn't make her ill—'

'How do you know?' he demanded. 'Medical science is coming round more and more to the belief that stress can bring on illness.'

She gazed at his bowed head, seeing the lines of fatigue cut deep into his face, and her throat tightened.

'I don't regret that we made love,' she said with difficulty. 'I wish Jodie hadn't found us like that, but you'll never make me regret it.'

He said nothing and her mouth suddenly felt dry. 'Ethan…Ethan, do you regret making love to me?'

His head came up at that but before he could speak the

door of the waiting room swung open and Dr Kaufmann appeared, his normally taciturn face wreathed in smiles.

'I have good news for you, Dr Flett. We are moving your daughter out of the isolation ward this morning.'

Ethan gazed at him blankly for a moment, then a blinding smile lit up his face. 'You mean…you mean…?'

'*Ja*, she is out of danger at last.'

Ethan grabbed the doctor's hand and all but shook it off. 'I don't know how to thank you. I don't know what to say except thank you!'

'Is she all right?' Kate asked anxiously. 'Her heart—her lungs?'

'I'm afraid there is some evidence of bronchiectasis— scarring to her lungs,' Dr Kaufmann replied, 'but luckily her heart is not damaged.'

'How soon will she be able to travel, Doctor?' Ethan asked. 'I'd like…I very much want to take her home.'

Dr Kaufmann frowned. 'Three weeks—it could not be any sooner than three weeks. She will have to stay in hospital for another week so we can continue her antibiotics intravenously, then I would advise at least two weeks of complete rest and relaxation before you subject her to a plane journey.'

Ethan nodded.

'Can I see her?' Kate asked. 'When she's moved to the ordinary ward, I mean.'

Dr Kaufmann looked suddenly uncomfortable. 'I'm afraid she does not wish to see you, *fraülein*. She was very specific about that.'

Kate turned away quickly so he couldn't see the tears that sprang into her eyes. She'd hoped, prayed, that Jodie would get well, and she'd hoped and prayed, too, that the girl might relent, might be prepared at least to meet her halfway, but it was clearly not to be.

'Kate, I'll speak to her,' Ethan said as soon as the doctor had gone.

'It doesn't matter,' she said, her voice clogged with un-shed tears. 'All that matters is she's all right. She'll need careful nursing, of course, when we get back to Malden—'

'Kate, about going back to Malden,' he interrupted, clasping her hands tightly between his own. 'Jodie…she's had so much tragedy in her short life, so much unhappiness. I love you, I love you very much, but I think perhaps it might be better if you didn't stay on as her nurse when we go back.'

'Not stay on?' she said, her heart faltering.

'I don't mean we shouldn't see each other any more,' he continued hurriedly. 'Of course we'll see each other. I'll come down to London when I can but seeing you every day at Malden, feeling the way she does, having that con-stant reminder…'

'Is that all I am?' she said bleakly. 'A constant re-minder?'

'You know what I mean, Gemma. We need to give her time to adjust, time to come to terms with things.'

Slowly she pulled her hands free, and her voice when she spoke sounded like somebody else's. 'You just called me Gemma.'

'Did I?' he said in surprise. 'I'm sorry, I don't know why I did that.'

But she knew.

He didn't love her. If he loved her he wouldn't have distanced himself so effectively from her over the past week. If he loved her he wouldn't be sending her away with vague promises of coming down to London to see her. And if he loved her he wouldn't be feeling guilty about making love to her or have called her by his dead wife's name. Jodie had been right. He was still in love with Gemma, he probably always would be.

'Kate—'

'I think—if you don't mind—I might go back to the

chalet,' she said swiftly. 'Have a proper shower, get a change of clothes.'

'That's a good idea,' he replied, then gazed at her a little uncertainly. 'Kate—you do understand, don't you, about Malden?'

'Oh, yes,' she replied with scarcely a tremor. 'I understand perfectly. *Auf wiedersehen*, Ethan,' she added softly as he made his way to the door, but he heard her and turned with a smile.

'Don't you mean *bis bald*—see you later?'

She nodded but she knew what she meant. He'd bought the return tickets on the day Jodie had been taken ill and she meant to use hers. She couldn't stay on here, knowing neither Jodie nor Ethan wanted or needed her. She had to go home, and go home now, before her heart was completely broken.

CHAPTER TEN

ETHAN sighed as he gazed out through his rain-spattered study window. He always found October a particularly depressing month and this year it had seemed even more so. The constant heavy rain they'd been experiencing for the past few weeks hadn't helped, of course, but it wasn't just the weather. Nothing had been the same since they'd come back to Malden, nothing had felt the same.

He sighed again as he walked slowly back to his desk and sat down. Once—oh, it seemed like a lifetime ago— he had looked on this house as a haven, a safe retreat from the outside world, and yet now, increasingly, it felt almost like a prison.

'Are you busy, Dad?' Jodie asked as she stuck her head round the study door.

Swiftly he turned over the blank sheets of paper in front of him and managed to smile. 'Hard at it, as you can see, sweetheart. Something you want?'

'How's your book going?' Jodie asked, coming forward a step.

'Great—really great,' he responded, edging his overflowing waste-paper basket under the desk with his foot. 'Was it something in particular you wanted?'

His daughter pleated the edge of her sweater awkwardly and shook her head. 'It doesn't matter—it can wait.'

'There's no time like the present, Jodie,' he said as she turned to go. 'Spit it out.'

'But you're busy—'

'I'm never too busy to see you, you know that,' he said firmly.

For a moment she hesitated and then, to his surprise, she

squared her thin shoulders, as though she'd come to a decision.

'Dad, I've got something to tell you—something I should have told you before—but before I tell you I want you to promise you won't go ballistic and yell at me.'

He smiled. He didn't think he could ever be really angry with her ever again after all the time she'd spent in hospital in Austria. 'Of course I won't get angry with you, Jodie. So, what awful, appalling thing have you done?'

She gazed at him silently for a moment, her blue eyes still far too large for her small face, then took a deep breath.

'Dad, do you remember the day before I got sick when I went down to Kitzbühel and came back later and…and had that row with you and Kate?'

Remember it? he thought grimly. He thought it would be etched on his memory for ever.

'Yes, yes, I remember,' he murmured.

'Well, that morning, after Kate started me on my antibiotics, I…I coughed up a little blood.'

'You did *what*?'

'You promised you wouldn't yell at me,' she protested, taking a step back as he rose to his feet. 'You said you wouldn't go ballistic—'

'That was before I knew what you were going to tell me,' he exploded. 'Why didn't you say something—why the hell didn't you tell Kate, or Rhona, or me?'

'Because I knew you'd stop me going down to Kitzbühel and I wanted to see Franz,' she replied defensively.

'And the very next day you went out and played two sets of tennis with him,' he groaned. 'Oh, Jodie, how could you have been so stupid!'

'I didn't intend playing,' she said, 'but Franz and I'd had such a row the day before and I wanted to show him that just because I had CF that didn't mean I was a…a liability or a drag. I know it wasn't the brightest thing to do—'

'You can say that again,' he declared angrily. 'Why

didn't you tell us about the blood right away? If you'd told us we could have got you into hospital earlier and you might not have been so ill.'

'I didn't want to go to hospital. I wanted to see Franz. I thought...' She paused and two large tears slid slowly down her thin cheeks. 'I—I thought he l-loved me, Dad.'

'Oh, sweetheart, don't,' Ethan said, striding quickly across the study towards her, his mouth twisted. 'Please, don't cry.'

'All that time I was in hospital, and then afterwards when I was convalescing in the chalet, he never came to see me once,' she sobbed into his chest. 'And now... We've been home nearly two months, and he hasn't even sent me a postcard. I know we had a row, I know I said a lot of things I shouldn't have, but you'd think he could have sent me one measly postcard.'

'Oh, Jodie, I'm sorry, so very sorry,' he said huskily, 'but I'm afraid you're just going to have to accept that sometimes...sometimes you can love someone very much but all the wanting and the wishing in the world can't make that person love you back.'

Hesitantly she raised her tear-stained face to his. 'You miss her, don't you—Kate, I mean?'

His arms tightened momentarily round her and he swallowed hard. 'Yes, I miss her.'

'And that was all my fault, too,' she continued, her voice trembling. 'She went away because of me, she left because of the things I said.'

'It doesn't matter any more, Jodie,' he said gruffly.

'But it does,' she protested, taking the handkerchief he was holding out and blowing her nose. 'I was so angry that day. Franz had been all over Marta like a rash, laughing and joking with her, ignoring me, and then when I came back... I thought you'd forgotten all about Mum, or that maybe you hadn't loved her as you'd always said you did.'

'Jodie, I will always love your mother.'

'But—'

'Sweetheart, listen to me,' he said as she stared at him in confusion. 'Do you love me?'

'You know I do.'

'But you love Franz too?'

'It's not the same—'

'No, it isn't, and that's just the point,' he interrupted gently. 'Jodie, there are many kinds of love. There's the love I have for you, the love I have for Kate, and the love I had for your mother. Your mother will always hold a very special place in my heart, and if she'd lived I know we would have grown old together. But she didn't live, and when I met Kate I thought…well, I thought I'd found someone who could make me happy again. Was that so very wrong of me?'

She shook her head tearfully. 'I'm sorry, Dad.'

'It doesn't matter any more, sweetheart,' he repeated.

'If she'd truly loved you, she would have stayed, wouldn't she?' Jodie said, gazing up at him uncertainly. 'I mean, she can't *really* have loved you, or surely nothing I said would have made her go away?'

'I guess not,' he replied, his eyes dark.

'Dad—'

'I have to get on with this book of mine, Jodie,' he interrupted swiftly, 'so, unless there's something else, scoot.'

She half turned to go, then paused.

'You'll always have me, Dad,' she said hesitantly. 'I'll always love you.'

'I know you will, sweetheart,' he said, his throat closing as he hugged her. 'Now, off you go or my book is never going to be finished.'

She went with clear reluctance and Ethan almost called her back, but he didn't want to admit even to his daughter that no matter how often he'd rung Kate she'd never answered the phone. All the letters he'd sent had come back unopened, and when he'd finally sneaked down to London in desperation, it had been to find Kate's flat all closed up.

'She's gone away,' her neighbour had told him with a meaningful look which had suggested that men like him should be hung, drawn and quartered, preferably slowly.

Gone where? he'd demanded to know, but the woman had promptly closed her door on him, and he'd gone home, and waited, and hoped, but—like Jodie—he hadn't even received so much as a measly postcard.

Where had he gone wrong? he wondered. Had he made her feel pressurised by saying they should get married when maybe she wasn't ready yet to make that kind of commitment? Had his love-making been too ardent, too passionate, and he'd frightened her without realising it?

Or was Jodie right, and the simple, unpalatable truth was that Kate didn't love him as he loved her and he was simply going to have to accept that fact.

'You look absolutely appalling,' Andrew said bluntly as Kate sat down opposite him and accepted a menu from the hovering waiter.

'Why, thank you, Andrew,' she replied dryly. 'I know I can always rely on you to say something to make me feel better.'

'But it's true,' he declared. 'Spending six weeks with Aunt Phyllis in her dreary cottage in Shropshire doesn't seem to have done you much good.'

It hadn't. She'd read a lot, walked even more, but nothing had erased the memories she wanted to erase, and eventually she'd been forced to acknowledge that nothing ever would.

'How is the old girl?' Andrew continued. 'Batty as ever?'

'Aunt Phyllis isn't batty,' Kate protested. 'She might be a little eccentric—'

'Kate, anyone who keeps all her life savings in a hat box

under the bed is batty. Anyone who spends her time knitting scarves for the horses in the field next to her house is batty.'

It was true, she did, but when Kate had turned up on her aunt's doorstep, unannounced and uninvited, Phyllis had merely eyed her shrewdly, shaken her head and asked no questions, and for that tactfulness she'd always be grateful.

'So what are you going to do now?' Andrew asked once the waiter had taken their order.

'Get another job, of course,' Kate replied briskly.

'I think you might find that considerably harder than you imagine,' he observed. 'There's a recession on, you know, and I don't suppose Dr Flett will be willing to give you a reference after you ran out on him.'

'I did not run out on him,' she replied, colouring slightly under his sceptical gaze. 'I...we just decided it wasn't working out.'

He shook his head. 'Well, I'm not the kind of man to say I told you so...'

Like heck you're not, Kate thought angrily, very grateful they were in the middle of a crowded restaurant because it was the only thing which was preventing her from slapping the smug, sanctimonious look off her brother's face.

'Andrew, I made a mistake—it didn't work out—so can we just drop the subject?' she said sharply, before he could launch into one of his lectures.

He looked slightly taken aback, then rallied. 'I'd be only too happy to drop the subject, but getting another job—'

'I have several interviews lined up,' Kate interrupted. 'In fact, I had one this afternoon.'

'How did it go?' her brother asked curiously.

'Very well,' she replied with scarcely a blink.

And it had gone very well—to start with.

'You seem to be exactly the kind of nurse we're looking for, Mrs Rendall,' Anne Robinson of the Robinson Nursing Agency had said with a smile as she'd read through Kate's application form. 'In fact, there's only one tiny little point I'd like to query with you. Since you left the Birnham Infirmary three years ago you seem to have done nothing but temporary supply work—a week here, a month there. The longest you've stayed anywhere was when you worked for this Dr Flett and yet you haven't put his name down as a referee. Would there be any particular reason for that omission?'

And that, Kate remembered, squirming inwardly, had been when the whole interview had gone down the tube.

In fact, it had been at that point that every interview she'd had since she'd returned to London had gone down the tube. As soon as she'd admitted that it was highly unlikely that Dr Flett would furnish her with a reference the smiles had become fixed, and she'd known as she'd walked out of the thickly carpeted offices that her application form was being quietly binned.

'It's not going to be easy, getting another job without a reference,' Andrew commented as if he'd read her mind. 'Couldn't you write to Dr Flett—spin him some tale about having to leave unexpectedly because of a family crisis?'

'Andrew, if you're only ever going to ask me out for a meal so you can lecture me about what I should and shouldn't do, I think I'd prefer to go hungry,' she retorted.

'But—'

'Dr Flett won't give me a reference,' she continued firmly, 'so can we just enjoy our meal and stop talking about him?'

That Andrew would clearly have liked to argue with her was obvious, but their meal had arrived, and if there was one thing her brother liked more than a good argument it was good food.

Kate wished she'd been in the same fortunate position. As far as she was concerned, the meal could have consisted of the most perfectly cooked food imaginable but her appetite had gone. Her appetite always disappeared when she allowed herself to think about Ethan Flett.

He wouldn't give her a reference. Any man who hadn't even bothered to phone or write to her since she'd returned home wasn't going to put pen to paper to give her a glowing testimonial. Granted, he couldn't have spoken or written to her directly as she'd left for Shropshire almost as soon as she'd got back, but she'd told her next-door neighbour to forward her mail and the only things that had come had been bills and circulars.

Face up to it, Kate, she told herself as she toyed with her meal, Jodie was right. He doesn't love you, he didn't ever love you. He only wanted you as a nurse for his daughter and when she objected to his choice he wanted to get rid of you.

'Let me know how you get on with the job search,' Andrew said as they stood outside the restaurant, waiting for his taxi. 'I'll put out a few feelers for you but with this recession on...' He sighed and shook his head. 'Perhaps you should think about retraining as something else. Secretaries are always in demand, though your age might count against you. Employers are looking for young staff nowadays and you're thirty next month, aren't you?'

'Your taxi's here, Andrew,' she said tightly, unfurling her umbrella as it started to rain again.

'You're absolutely positive I can't give you a lift home?' he said as he got in.

She shook her head. Walking home in a monsoon would be infinitely preferable to even one more second of her brother's company, and she knew if he gave her a lift he'd expect to be invited in, and once in she'd have the devil's own job to get rid of him.

'I have things to do before I go home, Andrew,' she lied, 'but thanks for the offer.'

It was an offer she almost found herself wishing she'd

accepted, however, when she slowly began to trudge her way home.

She'd scarcely walked a few blocks when the rain became a deluge, and with the world and his wife using umbrellas as though they were lethal weapons it was actually a relief when she finally turned the corner into Harrier Street. For once she was actually glad to be back to her basement flat, instead of experiencing the customary pall of depression which usually settled on her shoulders when she returned to the dingy flat she called home.

Quickly she ran down the stairs, shaking her umbrella as she went, and didn't see the man sheltering under the staircase until she almost collided with him.

'If you're thinking of mugging me, I haven't got any money,' she said, her heart racing. 'And if you're thinking of doing anything else, I should warn you that my husband is a policeman—'

'Kate, it's me,' the figure said quickly, stepping out from the shadows. 'Ethan.'

'Ethan?' she echoed faintly. 'But what—why—'

'Kate, can I come in for a minute?' he interrupted as she gazed up at him in amazement.

'Of—of course you can,' she stammered, fitting her key into the lock with trembling fingers, her mind in a whirl. 'The flat's a bit on the chilly side as I've been out all day, but it won't take me a second to light the gas fire, and then—'

'Kate, is Jodie here?'

'Jodie? Why in the world would you think she'd be here?' she said, turning to him in confusion, only to see his shoulders slump. Real fear clutched at her heart. 'What is it—what's happened?'

'She left Malden yesterday morning and was last seen at Alnwick, getting on the London train.'

'Oh, Ethan, no,' she whispered. 'Her medication—did she take any of her medication with her?'

'She took everything but the fridge it was stored in, thank heaven, but I hoped...' His face twisted. 'She left a note, saying she was going to fix everything, and I thought—I hoped—she might have come to you.'

'We didn't exactly part on friendly terms in Austria, if you remember,' she said gently. 'Have you checked with her friends?'

'She hasn't got any friends at home—you know that,' he said bleakly as he followed her into the sitting-room where she lit the gas fire. 'There's no one but Di and her husband, and they're both away in Tuscany right now.'

'Franz,' she said suddenly. 'He enrolled at London University this autumn, didn't he? Could she have gone to him?'

He shook his head. 'He's the last person she would want to see, believe me.'

'It's still worth asking him, isn't it?' Kate said, reaching for the phone book.

'I guess so,' he muttered, but as he turned away from her to stare at the gas fire she let out an exclamation as raindrops scattered from his coat onto the carpet.

'Ethan, you're soaked through. Give me your coat—'

'I'm fine—'

'Don't argue with me—just give me your coat and sit down,' she insisted, hustling him to a seat. 'Have you had anything to eat today?' she continued, noting the pallor of his skin, the dark shadows under his eyes. 'You haven't, have you?'

'Kate, I'm OK—'

'You're anything but,' she retorted. 'There's some soup in the kitchen, just waiting to be warmed up, and you're going to sit there and swallow it if I have to force it down your throat.'

'Jodie—'

'Getting sick isn't going to help us find her, Ethan.'

A ghost of a smile appeared in his tired eyes. 'You know,

that's only one of the things I've missed about you—your bossiness.'

'Well, you ain't seen nothing yet if you don't do as you're told,' she replied, considerably flustered. 'The soup won't take a minute, and while you're eating it I'll phone all the halls of residence and see if we can find out where Franz is staying.'

Swiftly she made her way to the kitchen, but as soon as she'd put the soup on to heat she leaned against one of the worktops and closed her eyes.

Why did Jodie have to run away now, bringing Ethan back into her life when she'd been trying so hard to forget him? Why did he have to suddenly appear out of the blue, effectively destroying in one swift moment the fragile shell she'd been trying to rebuild around her heart?

And he looked so awful, she thought as she reached for a bowl and spoon. He must have lost at least a stone in weight, and though she knew he was worried to death about Jodie he couldn't possibly have lost so much weight overnight, nor could the fresh lines she'd noticed on his forehead have appeared so quickly.

Stop it, she told herself as she began buttering some bread. Stop worrying about him, stop caring about him. He didn't care about you when he told you he didn't want you working at Malden any more. He didn't care about you when he didn't phone or write. You have to help him find his daughter but that's where your involvement ends unless you want to be hurt all over again.

But when she went back into the sitting-room and saw him sitting hunched over the fire all her resolve crumbled. When she watched him spooning soup into his mouth with hands that trembled while she telephoned the halls of residence, her heart seemed to die within her.

'He hasn't seen her?' he said when she finally tracked down Franz.

She shook her head.

'It's not quite hopeless,' she said quickly, seeing the despair in his eyes. 'He's going to ring Marta—'

'Jodie wouldn't go to Marta if she was the last person on earth,' he interrupted.

He was right, of course, but she'd run out of options, and she desperately wanted to give him hope.

'Ethan—'

'Why did you leave, Kate?' he said suddenly. 'Why did you run away?'

'I didn't run away,' she protested. 'I—I simply left to come home.'

'Without a word of warning or an explanation as to why you were going?'

She coloured slightly under his steady gaze. 'I left a note—'

'"I'm leaving because I think it's best for all concerned,"' he quoted. '"I've caused enough trouble between you and Jodie as it is and I don't want to cause any more." What kind of explanation is that, Kate?'

'An honest one,' she replied quietly.

'And was it honest of you not to reply to any of my letters?' he continued. 'Or did you simply not have the courage to meet me face to face, and tell me it was all over between us?'

'Letters?' she echoed, bewildered. 'Ethan, I didn't—'

'The one thing that stopped me from phoning the police and reporting you as a missing person when I found your flat all locked up was your neighbour, telling me you'd gone off with a suitcase.'

'You came down to London to see me?' she gasped.

'Kate, I phoned Gunther in Austria, thinking you'd gone there.'

She shook her head in amazement and confusion. 'But I didn't get any letters from you. Netta said there were none.'

'Netta?' he queried.

'Netta Ferguson. My next-door neighbour.'

'Small, dumpy woman, overrun with cats?'

'I wouldn't exactly describe her in those terms...' Kate couldn't help but smile '...but it certainly sounds like Netta. When I went away to Shropshire I asked her to send on my mail and there was never anything from you.'

'Kate, I wrote to you every day,' he declared, his eyes fixed on her. 'When you didn't reply, when you sent all my letters back, I thought...I thought it was your way of telling me you'd made a mistake, that you didn't love me.'

She had to ask, she had to know, and she swallowed hard. 'Would that have mattered to you?'

'Mattered?' he exploded. 'Kate, I'd asked you to marry me—damn it, woman, I'm in love with you!'

Unconsciously she shook her head. 'I think you might be fond of me—'

'Fond of you?' he echoed, his face stunned.

'And I can't blame you for thinking that if you married me you'd have a companion and a nurse to look after Jodie—'

He let out a long, low expletive that left her blinking.

'All right,' he said, thrusting a hand through his hair and making it even more dishevelled than it was already. 'Who spun you that load of old rubbish?'

'Ethan, I'm not condemning you, criticising you,' she said. 'I understand why you acted as you did—'

'Who spun you that load of old rubbish?' he demanded again.

'Jodie told me part of it. Oh, Ethan, don't be angry with her,' she said quickly as he swore again. 'I'm glad she told me the truth.'

'Kate, listen to me,' he said, coming across to her and grasping her hands firmly between his own. 'Do you think I would have made love to you the way I did if all I'd wanted was a nurse and a companion? Do you think I'd have phoned every Andrew Rendall in the telephone directory, looking for your brother, before I remembered that Rendall was your married name?'

'You phoned every Andrew Rendall?' she said faintly. 'But why?'

'I wanted to find you, to talk to you, to find out what I had done to make you run away from me.'

His blue eyes held such tenderness, and she wanted to believe him, but the doubts were still there, the memories of what had happened at the hospital were still here, and she stared down at her hands, unable to meet his gaze.

'Ethan, if you love me as you say you do, why did you shut me out at the hospital?'

He sighed. 'Kate, for four years I've had to deal with every crisis that hit Jodie on my own. With Gemma dead there was nobody but me to deal with it, and the only way I could survive was to turn that worry inside, to keep the panic and the fear I felt locked within me. It was wrong— I realise it now—and if you hadn't run away—'

'I wish you'd stop saying I ran away,' she interrupted vexedly. 'I did *not* run away.'

'Ran away—left—we won't quarrel about semantics now that I've found you again,' he said softly, but when she said nothing he tilted her chin with his fingers so she was forced to look up at him. 'There's something else, isn't there—something else that makes you think I don't love you?'

She tried to evade his piercing eyes but it was no use and eventually she muttered, 'You called me Gemma.'

'What?' he said in confusion.

'That last day in the hospital—before I left—you called me Gemma.'

'It was a mistake,' he exclaimed. 'It doesn't mean anything.'

'Doesn't it?' she said sadly.

'No, no, it doesn't. Kate, listen to me,' he continued, seeing from her eyes that she wasn't convinced. 'If you marry me—and, believe me, I'm going to do my level best to persuade you to marry me—there are going to be times when you'll hear me call out Gemma's name in the middle of the night. There may even be times when you'll whisper Simon's name, not mine, when we make love. It won't mean we don't love one another.'

'But—'

'Kate, we can't pretend we didn't love somebody else before we met, and I sure as heck wouldn't want to, but we've been lucky. We've been given another chance to love, and I want to grab it with both hands. I don't want to lose you—I won't lose you. I loved Gemma, I always will, but I love you, too. Not instead of, or in spite of, Gemma—I just love you.'

Tears filled her eyes and she blinked them away. 'Ethan, I do love you—I think I always will, but Jodie—'

'She didn't mean what she said. She was angry and upset about Franz. I know she's sorry for the things she said to you and she desperately wants you to come back.'

'Did she say that?'

He had the grace to look uncomfortable. 'Not in so many words, no, but—'

'Ethan, she isn't ever going to accept me, and I won't drive a wedge between the two of you.'

'Let me talk to her again,' he insisted. 'When…when we find her let me talk to her, but if she won't listen, if she refuses to come round, then we'll wait until she goes to college. We'll wait until she's married and has kids of her own if we have to, but somehow, some day, I'm going to marry you, Kate Rendall.'

Her eyes filled and as tears splashed down her cheeks she threw herself into his arms with a muffled sob. He rocked her gently in his arms and murmured silly, inconsequential things that sounded just wonderful.

'I can't stay,' he said at last. 'The police—they said if

Jodie wasn't here, if you had no idea where she was—I was to go back and fill in a…a missing person form.'

'I'll come with you,' she said, getting to her feet, but as she reached for her coat the doorbell rang.

'Will I answer it for you?' he offered, and she shook her head.

'It'll be Netta. She's probably bringing round one of her vegetarian dishes for me to try, but don't worry. I'll get rid of her.'

It was her neighbour, her long grey hair tumbling out of her topknot as usual, her oversized overall spattered with clay from the pots she made for a living.

'Got something for you,' she declared in her usual terse fashion.

'It's very kind of you, Netta, but right now—'

'She turned up late last night. Did what I always do with waifs and strays—took her in.'

'Her?' Kate exclaimed, hope rising in her breast. 'Do you mean you have Jodie at your place—Jodie Flett?'

'Just said so, didn't I?' her neighbour replied.

Kate let out a low sigh of relief, then said anxiously, 'Is she all right? She has CF—'

'I know—she told me.'

'Her father's going crazy with worry.'

'I know—we saw him waiting outside your door.'

'You saw him?' Kate gasped. 'Oh, Netta, why didn't you tell him she was safe?'

'The kid told me not to. Said she only wanted to see you.'

Kate didn't know whether to kiss her plump neighbour or hit her, and a sudden thought came into her mind. 'Netta, the letters Dr Flett sent to me—'

'Sent them back as per instruction.'

'As per instruction?' Kate echoed faintly.

'Knew you didn't want to see him again—that's what

you said before you left. Very insistent, you were. I don't care if I never see Dr Flett ever again, you said.'

She had said that. She'd been so angry, so upset, that all she'd wanted had been to get away and try to rebuild her life.

'Where is Jodie now?' she asked. 'Is she still in your flat?'

Netta motioned over her shoulder, and as Kate peered into the dark she saw a small, frail figure standing uncertainly by the stairs to the basement.

'Jodie—oh, Jodie!' That was all she managed to say before the girl hurled herself towards her.

'I'm sorry—so sorry,' she hiccuped as Kate held her tight. 'I've made such a mess of things—'

'Come inside—you're getting wet,' Kate urged. 'Netta—'

'Done my bit,' she replied. 'Be on my way. If you need any help just holler.'

And with that she was gone.

Quickly Kate ushered Jodie along the hall to the sitting-room and then made for the kitchen herself to allow Ethan some privacy for his reunion with his daughter.

Within minutes, however, the kitchen door was thrown open and Jodie stood there, her cheeks stained with tears but her face determined.

'I've explained everything to Dad, and now I want you to listen,' she said quickly. 'The things I said to you in Austria—I didn't mean them—'

'Jodie, it's all right,' Kate said quickly, seeing Ethan appear in the corridor behind his daughter. 'You were upset, and we all say things we don't mean when we're upset.'

'Kate, my dad told me a little while ago that some-times…sometimes you can love somebody very much but that doesn't mean they have to love you back. Dad…' She paused and looked round at him and he nodded. 'He does love you, I know he does, so do you think...maybe if you tried really hard, you might grow to love him, too?'

'Grow to love him?' Kate repeated, her voice trembling.

'I know he can be bossy, and overbearing at times,' Jodie continued hurriedly, 'and he's not handsome like Herr Zimmerman was, but in a good light he's quite presentable and he can be quite funny when he wants to be.'

'Well, Kate?' Ethan asked as he came into the kitchen, his eyes holding hers with warmth and love. 'Do you think you might learn to love a man who's bossy and overbearing, and only just presentable in a good light?'

'I think...I think I might just be able to,' she whispered, her voice choked with emotion.

'Oh, brill!' Jodie exclaimed as her father took Kate's hand in his and held it tight. 'So everything's going to be all right now, is it? You're going to come back with us and marry Dad, and be happy?'

'Yes, Jodie,' Ethan replied, raising Kate's hand to his lips and kissing it. 'She's going to come back to Malden and marry me, and we're all going to be very happy.'

'Oh, brill!' Jodie repeated, clapping her hands with delight, and as Kate smiled across at Ethan she thought she couldn't have agreed with her more.

MILLS & BOON®

*M*akes
any time special

Enjoy a romantic novel from
Mills & Boon®

Presents...™ *Enchanted*™ TEMPTATION®

Historical Romance™ ⚕ **MEDICAL ROMANCE**™

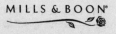

MILLS & BOON®

MEDICAL
ROMANCE™

HER FATHER'S DAUGHTER by Barbara Hart
New Author!

Dr Kate Marshall was covering a G.P. maternity leave in the
Lake District. She didn't know that Dr David Firth was a
partner—the man her father had thrown out of their house
She never had heard the whole story...

DIAGNOSIS DEFERRED by Rebecca Lang

Dr Laetitia Lane enjoyed emergency medicine, proud of her
achievements after a troubled past. Then Dr Grant Saxby,
the man who'd helped her straighten out, came back into
her life, and wanted to get to know her *much* better!

THIS TIME FOREVER by Joanna Neil

Dr Mollie Sinclair coped well with the rural practice until he
uncle fell ill. She didn't know her uncle had hired Dr Sam
Bradley, and having just been dumped by her fiancé, Molly
wasn't inclined to consider another man in a hurry!

MILLS & BOON®

MEDICAL ROMANCE™

COURTING CATHIE by Helen Shelton
Bachelor Doctors

Anaesthetist Sam Wheatley longs for a child of his own, but after two years with Cathie Morris, Sam is no closer to persuading her he's a good bet as a husband. Drastic measures are called for!

TRUST ME by Meredith Webber
Book One of a trilogy

Iain and Abby McPhee were having marital problems, and Dr Sarah Gilmour wanted to help. Then television star Caroline Cordell, a local girl, was killed—was it really an accident? As the forensic pathologist, it was Sarah's job to find out, and doing so might just bring Iain and Abby together again...

Puzzles to unravel, to find love

TWICE A KISS by Carol Wood
Book Two of a duo

Nick Hansen and Erin Brooks struck sparks off each other, but Erin refused to give up her fiancé, only to be jilted at the altar. Now Nick is returning to the Dorset practice...

Available from 5th May 2000

0004/03b

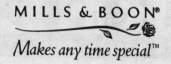

4 FREE

books and a surprise gift!

We would like to take this opportunity to thank you for reading this Mills & Boon® book by offering you the chance to take FOUR more specially selected titles from the Medical Romance™ series absolutely FREE! We're also making this offer to introduce you to the benefits of the Reader Service™—

- ★ FREE home delivery
- ★ FREE gifts and competitions
- ★ FREE monthly Newsletter
- ★ Exclusive Reader Service discounts
- ★ Books available before they're in the shops

Accepting these FREE books and gift places you under no obligation to buy, you may cancel at any time, even after receiving your free shipment. Simply complete your details below and return the entire page to the address below. *You don't even need a stamp!*

YES! Please send me 4 free Medical Romance books and a surprise gift. I understand that unless you hear from me, I will receive 6 superb new titles every month for just £2.40 each, postage and packing free. I am under no obligation to purchase any books and may cancel my subscription at any time. The free books and gift will be mine to keep in any case.

M0EA

Ms/Mrs/Miss/Mr ....Initials..
BLOCK CAPITALS PLEASE

Surname ....

Address ....

....

....Postcode................................

Send this whole page to:
UK: FREEPOST CN81, Croydon, CR9 3WZ
EIRE: PO Box 4546, Kilcock, County Kildare (stamp required)

Offer valid in UK and Eire only and not available to current Reader Service subscribers to this series. We reserve the right to refuse an application and applicants must be aged 18 years or over. Only one application per household. Terms and prices subject to change without notice. Offer expires 31st October 2000. As a result of this application, you may receive further offers from Harlequin Mills & Boon and other carefully selected companies. If you would prefer not to share in this opportunity please write to The Data Manager at the address above.

Mills & Boon® is a registered trademark owned by Harlequin Mills & Boon Limited.
Medical Romance™ is being used as a trademark.

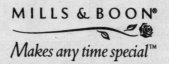